CALL ME WIZARD

CALL ME WIZARD

by Evelyn E. Smith

Coveting someone's wife and place in the world is an old, old story—except that the woman and the place Philip coveted were his own!

"What are you doing, scroyle?" Dorothea demanded, brandishing her ladle. Her elongated shadow cast on the wall by the leaping flames still gave Philip a tremor, although he'd been wed to the wench for nigh onto a decade. "You know right well 'tis you who should be a-mixing of this brew—'tis naught but a charm 'gainst the megrims, as any fool might contrive, for I ha' more weighty matters to which I should tend."

Philip had in truth been wondering why she had not noted his preoccupation afore. 'Twas queer she had let him be without hindrance for so long a space of time. Could she be up to some deviltry of her own? No, not Dolly-deviltry she was capable of, right enough, but 'twas not like her to be secret about her actures. For whom bad she to fear? There was no sorceress in the world who was her peer and, having a trace of royal blood in her veins, she was virtually above the law. Devil take the wench, why had he ever consented to espouse her? For 'twas monstrous hard to get shut of such a paragon.

"Jade me not, giglet!" he replied. "You're forever making plaint that I'm naught but a third-grade wizard! How can I pass the examination to better my rank if you'll not let me ply my own artifices?"

"Humph!" she sniffed, adding a pinch of powdered mummy to her brew. "Sith you're really desirous to be perfected in the mystical art, you could do no better than emulate me, 'stead of practicing your own paltry tricks—for, as all the world knows, I'm the most parlous necromancer in the realm."

"In *this* realm," Philip spoke before he thought.

She stared at him, and he could not fathom the look in her flat yellow eyes. "In *any* realm, rag," quoth she. "What d'ye mean, '*this* realm'?"

Philip glanced down at the pipkin in which he was mingling his own modest concoction. "Marry, I've heard talk," he said, somewhat weakly, "that there are other realms of existence—outside this one. Aye, and that there have been those from this realm who have visited another—"

"Twaddle!" Dorothea retorted, bending over her cauldron so that her long red hair concealed her face. "You'll never make a wizard, dribbling, if you'll not learn to distinguish 'twixt superstition and sorcery. Not that I fancy you'll ever attain even second rank, poor natural. Sorcery's a woman's work—it takes more of a closeness to nature, a practicality, than you or most men own."

Philip merely grunted in reply, for he feared he had said overmuch already. Superstition, push!

So there was something she did *not* know! He'd show the haggard wit-snapper the difference 'tween superstition and sorcery! For had he not come across an antique volume that gave the very receipt for the changement of existences writ out *in black and white*—with, moreover, the *exact* measurements for bat's blood and grated mandrake root and suchlike modern ingredients—and the proper spell to be chanted set down precisely in all the customary forms! And pictures, too, illustrating all these mysteries. Did that look like superstition, forsooth?

But he'd not tell her—let her discover it for herself when he was gone. Then she'd grieve over his loss when 'twould be too late. "Aye, weep your eyes out, my lady," he muttered. "I'll warrant me you'll ne'er find another spouse as lovesome as I—" " Eh?" Dorothea queried.

"'Tis naught," he replied hastily. "Merely a spell I was running through."

"Well, hold it to yourself, else it'll mingle with mine and who knows what strange and unnatural forces it might unleash? Sorcery's a serious thing, rogue. Y'must not slubber it."

"Aye," he agreed. "'Twould not be well."

But it was not for that reason he assented. It was rather that he did not want her to hear the spell he was chanting. For once he had learned that they existed, he had searched the various realms of existence in his crystal—and found another Philip Gardner marvelously like himself.

Now he gazed into the crystal, which he held concealed 'neath a fold of his palliament, and saw the image of his counterpart reflected therein. How frolicksome a jade was Nature—to fashion two men in the same assemblance, yet make one a handsome, hearty rogue and the other, though touch for touch the same fellow, a lank, pallid, peeled cullion.

Peeled . . . Philip felt his beard thoughtfully. Philip[2] had no beard—belike the poor twig was incapable of one. So his own brave valance was like to prove monstrous awkward. For he could not remove it ere he left or Dorothea'd be sure to take notice and impeach his motives therefor. He'd have to get it off afterward and the same for his robes . . . mortal strange attire they flaunted in that other realm.

But now that he had both spells pat, he'd transfer himself there. He looked into the depths of his crystal. Marry, but that was a plausive dame with whom Philip[2] was holding parlance. For shame, the rudesby had made her weep! Let her but tarry a bit and her estate would be bettered.

"I'll consolate you, my pretty wench," Philip murmured.

"What?" Dorothea said sharply.

"I did not address you, kicksy-wicksy," he snarled. "I but spoke to myself. Must I crave your leave to soliloquize?"

"If y'addressed yourself as 'pretty wench,'" she retorted, "you're even scanter of wit than I'd fancied . . . eh, Perkin?"

The cat miaued. Always agreeing with her, Philip thought resentfully—smoothing her and soothing her. Well, she might be his superior in sorcery, but he had never stooped to fawning on her like Perkin. And let her see how she fancied this second Philip whom he was substituting for his own sweet self in this existence—the Philip who made women weep. But what if she discovered forthwith that Philip[2] was not her own lusty spouse? Impossible. Had she not said herself she placed no credence in the other realms of existence? And with his magical arts—for he had more doctrine than ever the proud-stomached wench had supposed—he'd alter the form of the false Philip to resemble himself, the veritable Philip, even more closely than Nature's original design.

"Here, Perkin," Dorothea commanded. "Lave me this crucible."

The cat obediently licked it clean with his tongue. *As I have been doing in essence for this many a year,* Philip thought. *But I'll be her pet domestic no longer. She never thought I'd have the , audacity to quit her—that's twice she'll have been proved wrong. That is, if the spell does work . . .*

He checked to make sure he had an ample store of the mixture, in case the need should arise for him to depart from the next realm of existence incontinently . . . and his crystal ball . . . *and* his pocket *Grimoire.* He decided he had all the equipment he required, thought,

Farewell, Doll—mayhap now you'll realize what a rare treasure you had in me!"

And Philip disappeared from that realm of existence while Dorothea's back was turned. Her back was still turned when Philip[2] took his place.

The transfer had been virtually instantaneous, so that Philip[2] was only just aware that something odd had happened to him. He had blacked out and there had been an odd rushing sound in his ears—Philip[1] passing him in infinity—and now here he was in a strange room. No, not wholly strange—although it was entirely different, except perhaps in dimensions, for some reason it reminded him of his own living room.

The furniture, so far as he could make it out in the half-darkness, was massive and ornate, unlike the chaste simplicity of his own Swedish modern. And the smell here was different, too—in fact, he had never been conscious of any odor at all in his own quarters, although, as a scientist, he realized that one was never conscious of the distinctive odor of one's own person or one's own home-odors which have little to do with cleanliness or uncleanliness, but stem from variations in food habits, metabolism, cleansing agents and furniture polish.

In this room, it was impossible to avoid noticing an almost tangible cloud of what smelled like the more pungent chemicals, mixed with smoke, heavy perfume or incense, spices and a strong taint of decay. The fireplace in his living room had been a small genteel installation, used only for occasionally cultivating small genteel blazes designed solely for visual appeal.

Here was a huge fireplace, containing a roaring inferno that gave this room what little light it had. And there had certainly been neither a cauldron in his room nor a gaunt female figure in flowing robes stirring its contents and ululating pensively to herself: "Bat's blood, cat's blood, pickled capers-snake's tongue, drake's tongue, purge the vapors."

"There must be some logical reason for this," he told himself sternly, "as there is a reasonable explanation for everything. If I keep calm, I shall find out." He applied himself to calm thinking. "Since this lady is the only person in the room, she is the logical one to whom I should apply for information." An odd irrelevant thought—it occurred to him that she looked like one of those sackcloth-and-glamor witches drawn by that fellow Adams. Or was it Addams?

As he emerged into the ragged circle of light cast by the fire, the long amber eyes of the woman seemed to see for the first time. She was clearly *not* afraid. Her throaty contralto laughter played delicate arpeggios upon Philip's nerves. He couldn't help wondering whether, in the reversing roles of male and female that characterized the mid-Twentieth Century, he had not been the victim of a white slave gang. After all, his female students had found him attractive.

"I knew y'couldn't do it, geck!" the woman informed him with a visible gloat, waving her ladle in triumph. "Any fool could disappear for the matter of a minute, eh, Perkin?"

There was a yowl from the darkness where, beyond the reach of the firelight a pair of nitid green eyes regarded Philip[2] knowingly. It was only a black cat, virtually indistinguishable from the shadows, yet a memory of the stories he had read in his childhood before he decided that fiction was unworthy of the higher intellect stirred the hairs on the back of the man's neck.

"A witch," the memory whispered, "a witch and her familiar."

But this was absurd. He knew no such beings as witches existed. And why did he persist in feeling that, somehow, he was still in his own living room? Was all this his imagination? He had been studying too hard . . . overwork must have turned his brain. But one must be polite, even to the creations of one's own diseased brain.

"I—I beg your pardon, madam," he began, resisting the temptation to mop his brow, although the blast of heat that assailed him from the front provided ample justification. Behind him, cold lapped in icy waves at his spine. *It must be England,* he thought wildly. *No central heating.*

"Don't try your cozening airs on me, my lad!" the woman howled, waving her ladle so carelessly that part of the liquid it contained spattered on the faded Saruk, leaving a charred black circle and a stench where it fell. "You've failed, jolthead," she went on with evident relish. "Now you'll not deny that I am arch-sorcerer in this household or, in fact, any!"

"Madam," Philip[2] said , "I'm very much afraid you've mistaken me for someone else."

She stared at him. She was fairly young, he saw, and if the carroty hair that hung in elf-locks all around her thin face were arranged more becomingly, she might be rather attractive in an elegant angular *Vogueish* sort of way, for all her lack of grooming.

"Is this some jape?" the woman demanded. "D'ye think to gull me into supposing you've indeed journeyed to another realm according to your fond conceit? There *is* another realm to which I will dispatch you, if you persist in your fantastical behavior." Narrowing her eyes, she peered at him. "And what have you done with your beard, meacock?"

"Madam," Philip[2] said desperately, "I'm not whoever you think I am, I assure you. My name is. Philip Gardner. I'm a member of the faculty of—"

CALL ME WIZARD

"Of course your name is Philip Gardner. And Philip Gardner it was at the time , I wed you, ten years agone, when I was too young to know what I was doing."

"There's some mistake," Philip[2] persisted. "I'm not your husband—although I wish I were, I'm sure. My wife is much shorter than you and very much heavier." He had thought this would please her, but he was mistaken.

"Mock me with my meagerness, would you!" she cried. "How can you say you're not my husband then, for he's taunted me with naught else for the past nine years!"

"I—I meant no harm," he said hastily. "In my—where I come from, it's considered attractive to be slender. My wife starves herself all the time, hoping to get a figure like yours. But she'll never make it," he added, more to himself than to her.

"If you speak truth," she said, lowering her voice to more dulcet decibels, "and we are nowise akin, where would you say my own husband was then, eh, stranger from wherever you hail? For he's not here, you needs must agnize that yourself." She prodded him merrily in the ribs with her dripping ladle.

"H'm. I really don't know. Maybe you could tell me where I am now and then I could—" this was against all scientific principles, but he was quite at a loss—"make a guess . . ."

Had he traveled into the past somehow? But that was as illogical as anything else.

She stared at him. "Where you are now? Why, at our own dwelling at 379 Dulcamara Drive. Where else could you be, patch?"

Philip[2] blinked—379 Dulcamara Drive was his own address! So he *was* in his own living room. And yet he *wasn't*. How could that be?

He felt a little dizzy—from confusion, perhaps, or from the fumes that filled the room.

"May I sit down?" he asked mechanically, starting to do so in the nearest chair.

"Not there, measle!" she exclaimed. "Don't you mind the leg of that chair's of a mortal treacherous nature?" She laughed. "Aye, I still mind me of the day the Chief Warlock—the corky antick—came to tea and the wretched thing mammocked itself beneath him." She was overcome with laughter at the memory. The cat miaued with glee along with her.

Philip[2] smiled politely and sat in the chair she offered him. It was very hard. "Now I shall close my eyes," he told himself. "And when I open them, perhaps all this will be gone."

But it was still there. "It's no use," he sighed aloud, rubbed the chair arm. "I must be having a nervous breakdown . . . solid, technicolor hallucinations!"

The woman looked at him with concern. "To say sooth, knave, you don't look well. I'll compound you some phthysic in the twinkling of an eye that will oust the evil humors that beset you. First I'll empty the cauldron—" to his amazement, she poured the contents of the pot, which must have held at least four gallons, into a dram bottle—"and Perkin will clean the ladle like a good lad." The cat licked the spoon and smacked his lips ecstatically. "And then I'll set to work on a draught for you, lover. Green mold I'll need, aye, and the chaudron of a goat—"

Philip' shook his head. "No, thank you—please don't bother. I feel all right, really I do. Physically, that is. Psychologically, it's evidently quite another matter."

"Your fashion of speaking is passing strange," she said suspiciously. Her eyes narrowed again. "I fancy I begin t'apprehend your game, my lad. Conveyance, eh?" Suddenly she was in a towering fury. "Mountebank! I could report you to the American College of

Sorcerers! You'd have your license taken away, you caney-catcher! You'd not even stay a third-rank drumbling wizard!"

Then she chuckled hoarsely, her good humor restored as quickly as she had lost it. "So, you thought you'd fashion quaint plans to visit your 'other realm of existence,' forsooth, disappear for a moment, come back with your face unrough and your hair gilded to the yellow 'twas when first we were affied—and a sad day that was for me, too! Aye, and when you'd return from your counterfeit journey, you fancied I'd coo like a turtle and sigh, 'What a wonderful wizard y'are, alder liefest.'

"Well, I'll not do't" she exclaimed. "You'll not colt me with your fantasies. I know you for my mate, bearded or no!"

"Realm of existence. . . ?" Philip[2] repeated slowly, frowning. Oh, no, it couldn't be that—was too fantastic a concept! He must be in the past! "I know this sounds awfully silly, but could you tell—me what year this is?"

"Why, 1953, of course." Her stare seemed to peel skin, tissue and bone away from his head, layer by layer, as if she sought to discover what lay inside. "And well y'know that, falsing wretch! I'm beginning to think you have gone clean out of your wits."

"So do I," he said, rubbing the chair arm again and taking a deep breath of the heavy air. "They'll probably send me to an asylum . . . unless this is one."

He looked about him critically. This wasn't his idea of an insane asylum—but some of them, he had heard, were very old-fashioned. Besides, if he were insane, things wouldn't appear to him as they actually were; they would be shaped by his own diseased imagining. Probably the woman was an involuntary creation of his subconscious. One never knows what horrors lie concealed in the depths of one's own mind. He wondered vaguely if this was the way he really thought of his wife—as a witch.

She came very close to him, so close that he could smell the sulphur and incense and musk that wreathed her person. "Fear not, rogue, you're all the husband I have—and I mean to keep you whiles you're restored to your good senses. D'you apprehend me?"

"Madam—"

"Call me Dorothea, dearest chuck," she crooned, plucking a spider off his shoulder. "Or Dolly if you will, as you did when first we courted." She came closer to him. "Y'know, honey mouse—I don't know but that I fancy you better without a beard."

This—what was happening—he knew he couldn't have imagined.

II

The room was similar in size and shape to the chamber he had just quit, but the furnishings, Philip[1] thought, were much less handsome—nay, they were not sightly at all. Their outlandish simplicity offended the eye and they lacked the richness of texture and magnificence of carved wood and parcel-gilding that made him delight in his own appointments.

Here were no opulent velvures and ornate brocades in deep and brilliant hues, Tyrian tapestries and golden (albeit somewhat tarnished) broideries laced with silver . . . but, instead, flat fustian stuffs in dull brown monotones. The whole place was not pleasing to him. There was entirely too much light and air for the good of the health and the atmosphere was too thin to be virtuous.

Moreover, a chill layover the chamber, and he suspected a draught. He was mortal sensitive to draughts. 'Twould be an ironical thing were an ague to carry him off from this plaguey realm. After all, he hadn't planned to tarry here perdurably—just long enough to give Doll a sound fright. Although whether the fright would come from the loss of her spouse or from the knowledge that she was not absolutely omniscient, he could not be certain. He began to be a thought sorry he had cast the spell after all.

The room was tenanted, for there sat the lovesome wench he'd espied in his ball, perched on a chair as fubsy as her own delicious person. She was perusing a slender tome with a flexible particolored cover. He hoped she was not another learned wench like Dorothea. A noise filled the room, but Philip[1] could descry no musicians nor even any arras behind which they might be lurking. Magic doubtless.

The dame glanced up with large hazel eyes. "Oh, there you are, Phil," she said. "I wish you wouldn't appear and disappear like that, honey. It makes me so nervous. Did you get the toaster fixed yet?"

"Sweet lady—" he began, but she gave him no chance to finish and he, having not yet devised what he would say, was content to let her speak. Her voice was low-pitched, monotonous as the room itself . . . but it fell graciously upon the ears of one accustomed to Doll's jangling tune.

"Oh, I *knew* you couldn't do it! I guess I'll have to take it to the repair shop again. 'What's the use of having a scientist for a husband,' I always say, 'if he can't do a thing around the house?'"

"Will't please you, peerless dame—?"

"Go ahead, be rude to me! I'm used to it. I've lived with you for six years—I can take anything by now."

"Aye, verily," Philip[1] agreed, hoping his vagueness would pass muster, for in truth, although he brained the words this wench used, queerly formed though they were, their import clean eluded him.

She peered up at Philip[1]. He realized that she was shortsighted as a moldwarp and could barely discern him. But he liked her limpid hazel orbs withal—and he much favored a wench such as this over one who saw all too well all too often.

"Why are you wearing your bathrobe in the middle of the day?" she demanded. "If there's anything sloppier than that, I don't know what it is. And you haven't shaved. Honestly, Philip, I don't know what's come over you."

Philip' seethed with righteous wrath. A churlish way to describe a brave beard that had taken considerable time and enchantment to gain its present magnificence. And what had his robe to do with a bath? On such slate occasions as he bathed, he always doffed his robe. But, he saw full well, both robe and beard would have to go, alas. Undoubtedly Philip[2] had appropriate garments which he himself could filch. Fortunately they were both of a size.

She looked at him expectantly, and he realized that it was his turn to say something. "Lady, I do assure you—" he began again.

"And why are you talking that way? Really, Philip, if you start trying to be funny, I don't think I can stand it." She began to blubber a little. "I m-missed my m-morning toast and you d-don't even care!"

The toaster must be a mightily important thing, for assuredly she'd not create a whoobub over some paltry pieces of scorched bread, which, moreover, it took no engine but a good roaring fire to prepare. And how was it that this well-favored creature made no use of her own spells to put it back into operation? Was she too orgulous to submit her necromancy to ordinary household use, or was it possible that she had no wizardry of her own? Push! Everyone knew—though he'd never have avowed it to Doll—that women were by far the more natural necromancers.

What the fair creature needed was soothing and he, as husband temporary, was the fellow to sooth her. Accordingly, he coyed her auburn hair with hands that, he was much distressed to note of a sudden, were more like dirty claws. He must pay more heed to his appearance. When he wed Dorothea, he had been a brave figure of a man—but slaving over a hot cauldron had done its fell work. Natheless, he was a young man still. He could feel it in his liver.

"There, there, sweet mouse," he murmured. "No need for weeping, I do protest."

She looked up at him, onion-eyed. "Why, Phil, sugar, you never did that before. At least you haven't done it for a long time."

He coughed. Confound that draught. "Aye, you have the right of it, chuck. I have neglected you, spotted snake that I am! I was too immersed in my—er—conclusions." What was a *scientist*, anyway? "I shall tty to make amends. This I do vow most solemnly."

She stared. "Why are you talking so peculiarly? What's come over you?"

He repressed the reasonable rejoinder that 'twas she who had the odd fashion of parlance, minding that, after all, he was but a guest in her realm and in her house, ignorant though she might be of the fact.

"I have been poring over some curious tomes of alien vintage," he offered, feeling this to be an adroit apologia. "Mayhap they have twisted my tongue . . . but by your leave, sweet lady—" he hastily diverted the subject—"might I address myself to the engine you call the toaster? I am not without some doctrine of my own."

She looked puzzled.

"Will y'lead the way, fair one?"

What *was* the wench's name?

"Turn the radio off first, honey," she said. "No use wasting electricity."

"The- radio?" He followed the direction of her gaze, saw it rested upon a species of light-colored wooden coffer from which a doleful dump issued forth. Could there be a group of minikin players inside? Fantastical—it must be some kind of engine. He gingerly touched one of the bosses that whelked from the device. Forthwith a lively air was added to the melancholy strain, creating a mortal jangle.

She clapped hands to her shelly ears. "*Philip!*" she cried. "You've turned on the phonograph! I *knew* it—you've been at the Scotch again. and after all your promises! 'Dora; you said, eighteen times if you said it once, 'I swear to you that I'll never touch a drop again' . . . Do you want to make a spectacle of yourself in class again, the way you did last week?"

"Aye . . . That is, nay," Philip[1] replied, pleased to have learned her name at last, but more captivated by the musical box. The top of the gimmer opened as if 'twere a lid. Inside, a disk whirled round and round, and from this the second noise had apparently come. Now a voice joined the cacophony, singing some merry air.

Dora reached over his shoulder and twisted one protuberance after another. With a click, the melancholy tune and the gay one ended successively.

"I don't know how you can fix a toaster when you're too drunk to turn off the radio, but you might as well have a shot at it. If the repair shop fixes it, we'll have to pay plenty . . . and we're practically broke."

Philip[1] shuddered. Was one broken on the wheel here for debt? He felt nervously within his robe to make sure he had not lost his supply of ingredients for the return spell, so he could flee if conditions became too perilous. They were there, right enough, in the small velvet bag suspended from his neck. But what if the trip had altered them in some wise, so that they would not act correctly? He could not tell without essaying them and, if he essayed, he would leave this realm, which he did not plan to do yet.

"Dame Fortune be kind to me," he breathed as he followed the Lady Dora toward a door on t'other side of the room. It had been an age, he mused, as he admired her tidy, silk-gowned curves bouncing before him, sith he'd inclipped any but a bag of bones.

At that moment, his conscience took it upon its meddling self to smite him. For had he not abandoned Philip[2], who was well-nigh his brother—indeed more than a brother, being his own very self—to that same bag of bones? Oh, well . . . Doll'd be more of a lesson to him than a book. But a *scientist*—that sounded as if he might be a learned wight. And a man of learning might be able to find his way back to his own realm of existence. Philip[1] had never mused over such a potentiality—want of forethought had always been his bane. Should the other return, especially at an inopportune occasion, there would be a rare gallimaufry!

Dora led Philip' into a species of laboratory, where she indicated a metal device that needs must be the toaster. Marvelous complicated, it appeared, but he could not account himself sorcerer and be baffled by any engine. There was bread inside. If all she listed was to burn it, why could she not do so over the fire? Then he looked about him and saw there was no fire.

"This realm must ha' branched off a long time agone, perdy," he mused, "for 'tis apparent that it holds no heritage from Prometheus."

"As I understand the matter," he quoth aloud, donning his professional mien, "this gimmer is not operating in the manner for which—twas fashioned."

Dora giggled agreeably. "Oh, Phil, you are a scream—even if you are drunk. Do you think you can fix it?"

She looked up at him hopefully. Her face was full and fair as the moon's. She was a sweet lady, and he recked not whether her lips were rubious from art or from nature. There'd be no harm in bussing his own german's wife, he thought, especially since the churl—according to his lady's plaints—had been somewhat sparing of caresses.

"You don't have to fix the toaster this very minute," she said breathlessly as she emerged flushed and a trifle disordered from his ardent embrace. "Funny," she added, "I don't *smell* any liquor on your breath."

"Nay, I must atone for my shrewish behavior of the mom." Tucking up his sleeves, he waved his hands over the toaster in the set movements.

"Whatever was dark
Now shall be light.
Whatever was wrong
Now shall be right."

CALL ME WIZARD

"But I *like* dark toast," she protested.

Philip[2] frowned. "I must have absolute silence during my spell," he ordered.

"Genie, warlock, witch, or mage,

Thaumaturge, savant or sage,

Necromancer, wizard, gnome,

Whatever spirit plagues this home,

Demon, kobold, imp or gbost or

Whoe'er you be, unspell this toaster."

He snapped his fingers. "Be operant once again."

The filaments in the toaster glowed a rosy red. Both pieces of bread shot to the ceiling and rebounded, an even golden-brown on both sides.

"Oh, Philip!" Dora sighed, clinging to him. "You're wonderful!"

Her person was warm and yielding in his arms. While her head was pressed against his bosom, he took the occasion to magick away his beard. 'Twas a woeful thing to have to do, but a small price to pay for the favor of so lovesome a damsel as this. No need to return to his own realm for another few days . . . or weeks . . . or mayhap even ever. After all, Dorothea had little need for him—she had her career.

He pulled aside a flap of his robe so he could get a glimpse of his own world in the crystal. Pity he could only see but not hear. What was that? Doll *embracing* the fellow? Could she really have been deceived into fancying such a frampold losel to be her own Philip? Well, 'twas his own craft that had bleared her eyes.

Had she any real perceptivity, she'd have known by now—but then hadn't he always said she was more sorceress than woman? Now this tender-hefted lady in his arms-she was all woman!

22

Dora looked up at him with worshipful eyes. "Darling, I'm sure nobody could have fixed the toaster as well as you did. Why, it works without even being plugged in!"

*

"Sip this, sweet lad," Dorothea said tenderly, offering Philip[2] a cup of reeking liquid. "Let's have no defiance—'twill bring the roses back to your cheeks. Of a truth, I've never seen you so pale I I wonder if 'tis the loss of your beard—" she touched his cheek with a cold hand—"for they say that the cutting off of a man's hair saps his mortal strength, as with Samson."

"Samson," Philip[2] repeated. Here was something he could understand. "Then you have the Bible?"

She stared at him. "Of a certainty we have the Bible. What d'ye take us for—savages? In truth, Philip, I begin to think y'are indeed sore diffused. Drink the electuary, man. 'Twill relieve you of your ecstasy and warm the cockles of your being."

Philip[2] drained the cup at a gulp. It wasn't bad at all—it was sweet and definitely contained alcohol.

"That's my good peat," she said approvingly. "I'd be loath t'have it go to waste, for it's a mighty clever concoction. Albertus and Agrippa themselves could not surpass me in contrivance. And a pretty penny th'elixir cost me, too, for toad's entrails come prodigious high these days. But there's naught too good for you, honey mouse."

Philip[2] gulped. He felt he should be sick, but strangely enough he seemed to feel stronger, more invigorated. And he wasn't shaking any longer. Odd how effective the power of suggestion could be.

The cat rubbed against him and he bent over to stroke it. It felt just like an ordinary cat. It purred just like an ordinary cat. Even an ordinary cat, he figured, could be trained to clean dishes. He must try it on a kitten when he got back to . . .

23

He throttled the thought. He didn't know where he was or how he could return.

Dorothea stretched and her black shadow on the wall stretched along with her. "Well, to work now . . . I spent all of yesterday and this morn soothing your evil humors. But woman's work is never done."

Crossing the room to a massive carved wardrobe surmounted by a grinning skull that lent—Philip[2] thought—a cheerful note to the room, she took out a long black cloak of some coarse material, which she wound about herself like a cocoon. Philip[2] watched with disapproval. Her clothes were unbecoming; he must get her to wear brighter colors and dresses that were made to fit her instead of a sack of flour. Put a little makeup on her face, fix her hair, dress her right and she'd ornament any magazine cover with distinction.

"I needs must quit you for the nonce, dearest chuck," Dorothea said, fastening the clasp of her cape. "The Lady Alison has need of a cunningly wrought love potion, such as only I have the art to make, for the men are marvelous afeared of the wench, despite her beauty . . . and she's too fine, forsooth, to come fetch it herself, despite the fact that I'm of higher estate than she." She looked at Philip[2]. "And now that I mind me of it," she added, "'tis as well that the luxurious giglet does not come herself."

"Can't you insist that she come?" Philip[2] asked.

"Now, sparrow, wouldst have me lose my license? Y'know that were I to refuse t'attend the bedside of a patient, I'd be violating the Merlinian Oath. What's amiss with your wits, rogue? For you too are bound by the oath, despite your inferior degree. Many's the time have I wondered why I wed a fellow practitioner of the mystical art, for 'tis better when a pair's interests are disparate, so that they do not clash—else the lower's always mortal jealous of the higher."

She sighed, then smiled at him. Her smile was very attractive. "Now mind the wares, sweet spouse."

She kissed him good-by—Philip[2] did not find the sensation at all unpleasant—and was gone. So confused was he that it took him a little while to realize she hadn't opened a door and walked out.

She had simply disappeared. Curiouser and curiouser. He wondered what laws governed this strange world to which he had been conveyed.

He went to the door and rattled its knob. It wouldn't open—yet he knew instinctively that no lock held it shut. And the windows were also tightly shuttered with the same—he could not bring himself to call it spell-device.

Whatever it was he was trapped.

III

"You'd better get dressed, Phil," Dora yawned. "You've got to go to class."

"Class?" Philip' repeated, sitting up reluctantly. "Am I a scholar, then?"

Certes, but they stayed students to a ripe old age on this plane. Could it be that the other Philip was his junior? But nay, sith they were the same man, logic must have them the same age—two and thirty. Well for him that learning was favored in this realm, for Philip[1] was himself a most authentical fellow.

"Of course, honey," Dora said gently, pushing him off the bed. "You're a scholar and a gentleman. Now hurry. Your students will be waiting."

"Oh, I apprehend you now! I am a pedant—a schoolmaster!"

"Philip," she murmured sweetly, patting his cheek, "we'll joke another time. My, how smooth your face is. Did you get an electric razor?"

"Ee—aye."

"Oh, do stop talking that way," she said gaily. "And hurry up and get dressed. If you keep on being late, Professor Brunschweiger will never renew your contract."

He pulled open the cupboard door and discovered strange and rare attire. Sith the more gorgeous raiment was much too small for him, he was forced to the sorry conclusion that the sober garments—better suited to a monk or a priest than a lusty young wizard—were the other Philip's.

A peduncle and garbed in such wise! he thought. *I'll warrant me he's a philosopher.* And his heart lightened, for he was not unskilled in divers philosophies and could make shift to instruct the young in their precepts.

26

Garbing himself in those garments least displeasing to the eye, he anointed himself from a pouncet box he found upon a chest of drawers and approached the bed to buss his spouse—or Philip[2]'s.

Dora sat up with a gasp of dismay. "Philip, enough is enough! You know very well you can't teach your physics class in a purple sport shirt and green slacks. And that's my best hat you have on, you idiot! I'm not sure whether you're trying to be funny or what!" She sniffed. "Is that *my perfume* you're wearing?"

Perdy, he had not thought a lady who was so generous of her favors to be so frugal of her possessions.

"I—I am sorry, my love," he faltered. "I fancied it to be my own."

"That's *not* funny! And I don't care if it *is* the modern fashion for men to wear cologne. I won't have you do it!"

"Yes, sweet mouse," he said meekly. He hoped she was not going to turn out a shrew after all.

"I let you pick out the furniture," she said. "You told me it was the latest thing and—"

"Was't *I* who sorted those paltry sticks of wood? I must have had a fit of the lunes. We'll make a roaring blaze of 'em on the morrow and procure something more suitable to our quality."

"Darling!" she said in delight. "I've hated them for years."

. . . *so I teach physics*, he mused as he arrayed himself in a sober suit of dark serge. *Have I left my own realm t'usurp the position of one of my arch-enemies, a physician?* Well, he'd show his young charges by his shrewd tutelage of what little avail was medicine 'gainst adroit necromancy.

Natheless, a leech needs must know somewhat of sorcery. The fear again attacked him that the other Philip might have sufficient art to transport himself back to his own realm—although in such case the wonder was that he had not appeared already. Moreover, if Philip[2] had not the skill, Dorothea might well aid him. Together they might fathom out the spell. Perhaps even now they were in the act of contriving it.

*

While Dora, sweet and gentle lady that she was, prepared their morning repast, he consulted his crystal ball. She had an engine, he noted, for laving the crockery. It occupied considerably more space than did Perkin, but 'twas also, he fancied, less likely to claw one about the ankles when wrathful.

But what was this he espied in the crystal? Dorothea—feeding t'other Philip a potion—a *love potion* by the look of it! This passed all comprehension. He'd go right straight back and demand . . .

"But softly now," he addressed himself. "Well she knows I'd be a-spying on her in the glass. She does this solely out of spite—for who could fancy yon lily-livered hilding. She thinks that when 1 view the pretty scene, I'll come hastening back to her. Well, I'll trick *her!*"

And that proved one thing, he thought cheerfully, as he partook of various odd but uncommonly palatable dainties—Dorothea knew not the spell, else she'd not resort to such devious means to retrieve her errant fere. So he was safe, for the nonce at least, from interruption by either Philip[2] or Dorothea at a—he clipped Dora tenderly as she aided him into his surcoat—parlous awkward time.

Sith he was not familiar with this new locale, he could not transport himself via the magical art to the university whither—he had found out from divers tricksy questions—he was bound. However, the driver of a gaudy-hued cart, powered by some mystic formula, gladly agreed to convey him to that place. Though Philip[1] had no gold upon him—Dorothea had always made certain of that—he found the knave to be much gratified by the gift of one of the bits of paper which he found in a leather case within his undercoat.

"Douhtless it has a very powerful spell writ upon it," Philip' reflected, "and 'tis mortal interesting to note the difference in the magical power of numbers from plane to plane of existence. For in my own world 'tis the odd numbers, particularly three, seven and nine, that are strongest—whereas, judging from th' inscription upon the charm I gave yon good fellow, 'tis the figure ten that is of mystic power here."

Philip[1] stared up at the Science Building. A goodly tower, but how would he find the apartment in which he was scheduled to begin his pedagogical duties amongst the foison with which this structure must be filled?

There was a giggle behind him. "Hello, Dr. Gardner," said a light voice.

He turned to find two maidens regarding him with worshipful expressions. Both bore weighty tomes and their attire, he noted with approval, was so fashioned as to give full emphasis to their budding charms.

"Aren't you coming up to class?" asked the other maiden, giggling at her own boldness. "You're.a little late, sir."

"Of a truth, I have not been well," Philip[1] replied. "I was seized by a species of rapture yestr'een, which well-nigh caused me to forgo today's instruction."

"Oh, that would have been terrible!" said the first damsel earnestly. "I come to class only to hear you." And she blushed.

"You still sound a little funny, Dr. Gardner," observed the second. "Probably something wrong with the nerve reflexes controlling your speech centers. We learned all about things like that in psychology. Here, lean on me and I'll help you up to class."

"No, lean on *me!*" quoth the first jealously.

"Perhaps," Philip[1] murmured, "if I could but avail myself of support from both, I would tax neither excessively."

Their arms were soft and round and warm, and both maidens smelled sweetly of some pleasing fragrance. He leaned a trifle more heavily upon them. They were sturdy lasses, well able to endure his weight.

And thus, supported by a fair damsel on either side, Philip[1] made an impressive entrance into Philip[2]'s classroom.

The apartment was recognizably a laboratory, though of a disagreeably aseptic assemblance. There should be corpses lying about for him to mammock, were he a leech—possibly, so point-devise was the chamber's arrangement, they were stored in the numerous cabinets set along the walls 'neath crystal-fronted cases. He himself liked everything to be laid out in plain sight, ready to hand. Should he decide to tarry in this quaint but appealing world, he would conform Philip[2]'s appointments to his own convenience and inclinations.

A goodly group of youths aspersed with a few maidens were seated before a low dais upon which stood a table. They did not rise as he entered and was tenderly led by the two damsels to a chair behind the table.

"Looka *him!*" remarked a clear male voice.

"Dr. Gardner isn't feeling well," one maiden explained. "You mustn't upset him."

"Layoff, goon," agreed the other, setting a large tome before Philip[2]. "Here's your textbook, Dr. Gardner."

Philip[1] passed his band over his eyes. Surely he should have reckoned aforehand on the other Philip's having some manner of occupation. "I fear me I am something mazed," he murmured.

"Prithee, gracious damsel, could you show me at what point the reading for today commences?"

There was a smothered guffaw from the male members of the class and whispering which he could not make out, but which his two fair mentors apparently could.

"He is *not* drunk!" One maiden stamped her foot. "He's sick. He shouldn't be teaching at all really, only he *insisted* on coming. There's something wrong with his speech centers—that's why he talks oddly."

"He works too hard," the other said in sepulchral tones. "He knocks himself out teaching you ungrateful ignoramuses . . . Here's the place, Dr. Gardner. We were going to start in on gravity, remember?"

"You know what gravity is, Dr. Gardner?" one of the boys said in a falsetto voice. "Whatever is dropped must fall down . . . *boom!*"

Philip[1] jumped despite himself, and all the youths laughed right heartily.

He was glad he could so facilely confound the forward knave. "Sirrah, that is false! Whate'er is dropped *may* fall down. On t 'other hand, it may rise."

He cleared his throat and spoke more resonantly now that he was assured of his ground. Fortunate that all that was required here was a simple spell. Were it some complicated formula that needed, say, a mandrake root, he'd not know where to get it in this humorous world—for the store he had concealed in the phylactery suspended from his neck was already mingled in the receipt for changing existences.

"Observe I lift this tome." He picked up the physics book. "I let it fall from my hand. It drops." The volume thumped to the floor. The class laughed—the youths again with more glee than the maidens.

"Now—" he turned to the two damsels who had guided him thither and who still hovered anxiously about him—"could I trouble you for some salt?"

And then he had a moment of doubt: did they *have* salt in this realm? Their hesitation did nothing to abet his faltering confidence. "S-salt?" quavered one maiden.

"But you don't use salt in physics."

"The chemistry lab will have some!" the other said sharply. "It's marked NaCl. Run next door and fetch some."

Philip[1] smiled weakly at the students. Supposing his spell didn't work here? He'd be the laughing stock of these princoxes. And if this spell did not operate, then neither would the concoction he wore in the bag around his neck. He would be lodged eternally in this lawless existence! Dora was a charitable wench, but he must not forget, Dorothea had royal blood—though there were thirteen between her and the throne.

The damsel was gone but for the space of a minute, yet it seemed like a mortal long stretch to him. She was back anon with a whitish powder. He touched the tip of his tongue to it warily. 'Twas salt, right enough.

"Now, fair maid—" he turned to t'other—"might I have a hair from your head? 'Tis only," he explained to the sulky salt-fetcher, "that I need a hair black as night and strong as silk."

Placing the hair and a pinch of salt atop the book, he intoned,
"Jet black hair will band
Salt as white as snow.
Tome, at my command,
Go where you must go."
He made the proper sign.

"I take it back," a male voice said distinctly. "He's not drunk—he's crazy." "And now," Philip! stated, casting a baleful eye at the rudesby, "again I let the book drop from my hand. But this time it does *not* fall."

And, indeed, the book rested motionless in the air without so much as a quiver. Philip[1] beamed. His magic worked excellently well in this realm. There was naught to fear.

A mortal hush fell over the classroom as he prepared to speak again.

"And, sith I so list, the book will rise to the ceiling—" the tome obeyed—"or, at my command, settle gently upon the floor sans sound."

The book floated gently to the floor, paused a moment, then lay down obediently. Every member of the class gazed at Philip[1] with respect, awe, admiration and such-like sentiments appropriate to his quality.

"And the lesson we are to derive from this," he added gently, "Is—take naught for granted, but keep a mind receptive of all things."

Long have I known, he told himself, *that I had some inclination as a pedant.*

One of the youths lifted his arm, obviously to attract the master's attent.

"What would you, good juvenal?" Philip[1] asked graciously.

"Could you—would you show us how you did—did *that* with the book?"

"Ay, marry, that will I with right glad heart." To call himself teacher, he needs must teach. "If there but were some means whereby I might inscribe the proper characters of the spell for all to view . . . Ah!" He took up a stick of some pale substance that rubbed off upon his fingers. "Haply I might use this white stuff to letter upon yon black panel?"

From the countenances of his students, he discovered he had surmised aright. 'Twas cleverness of apprehension as well as doctrine that made th'adroit necromancer.

"Be't so then. I shall write the characters upon this black—er—board, pronouncing them as I do so. And you shall repeat them aloud after me."

There was the clearing of a powerful throat from the back of the room. Previously Philip[1] had noted out the corner of an eye that a portly wight of advanced years had entered the room, but he had paid th' intruder scant mind, being too much occupied in confounding his forward charges. Now the stranger spoke and his voice was resonant with authority. "Just a minute, Dr. Gardner! Would you step into my office?"

The tone was the same that Dorothea employed when Philip[1] had bodged a brew (which, of course, happened only seldom-when). Apparently he had done something amiss. Well, there was naught to fear—did he find himself in aught that seemed dangerous, he had but to cast his spell and return to his own realm.

His fingers felt reassuringly in his bosom for the phylactery containing the ingredients and found—*nothing*. The little velvet bag was gone! Now he was imperiled indeed!

IV

Philip^2 felt afraid. Obviously Dorothea had not meant to trap him in the room—she had simply assumed that he would be able to leave the same way she had. As the Philip she thought he was probably could. But—was there any other way out? *Were* there streets outside? There must be—otherwise how could the house have an address? That was logical.

Come to think of it, where did he want to go? If he did get out of the house, he might lose himself so well that even Dorothea's arts—now look at him, he was beginning to take her magic powers seriously! But she *had* disappeared. He had seen her with his own eyes. Or, rather, he hadn't seen her . . . Maybe she had hypnotized him. Hypnosis was scientific. You could explain it logically.

Anyhow, he might get so lost even Dorothea wouldn't be able to find him. And so he might lose any chance of ever returning to his own existence, for here at Dulcamara Drive was his only connection with his former world.

Perkin, who had been rubbing ardently against his legs, now miaued importunately.

And then, "What ails you, varlet?" piped a voice behind Philip^2. "Can y'not see y'have a client awaiting you?"

Philip^2 whirled. A freckle-faced boy of eight or ten was regarding him with pale blue eyes. The child's clothes were strange—much more colorful and ornate than a boy would be caught dead wearing in Philip's own world—but they were obviously costly.

"I have need of your arts, sorcerer," he said with a lofty air.

"I will pay y'well for your contrivance and your discretion."

"Do you want a love potion, maybe?" Philip^2 couldn't help asking.

"Mock me not, wizard. Or, if you mock me, mock not my gold!" The boy smugly waved a small velvet bag. The jingling could easily be

35

that of gold. Philip^2 had not heard enough gold jingle in his life to be sure.

Spoiled child of the rich! he thought resentfully. He'd better do what he could to help the brat, however, for he needed Dorothea's assistance in getting back to his own world . . . although there was really no particular hurry. But he'd certainly not ingratiate himself with her by antagonizing the customers.

Pity he couldn't ask the boy how he had got into the room. But that would betray himself . . . and Dorothea. He wouldn't want to betray her. Finest woman he had ever known. And he'd have to leave her . . .

"What do you want, sonny?" he asked, clearing his throat of emotion. "Maybe I can help you."

"Of a sooth, sirrah, you speak fantastically," replied the child. "I'd heard tell that the sorceress's spouse was something lacking in wit, but I had not thought it so extensive a deficiency."

"If there's one thing I dislike," Philip^2 muttered, "it's a precocious child."

Then he realized that the little boy was no more precocious than a French child who speaks French; he was merely run-of-the-mill obnoxious.

"I like you not either," the child stated. "Moreover, for so delicate a matter as I have in mind, I fear you would not have sufficient artifice. Let me affront the sorceress herself, if you please," he commanded imperiously.

"Just what did you want done?" Philip^2 asked, annoyed. What, after all, could Dorothea do with her alleged sorcery that he could not surpass with his science? "Affronting me is quite enough for you, my boy."

"Well . . ." the child began hesitantly. "I should like some quaint gimmer, some clever and fantastical contrivance, that upon th'application of the proper spell would burst incontinently with a heartwarming clamor. 'Tis rather tedious at the pa'at my abode and I fain would inject some vivacity into the atmosphere. Meseems 'twould be a right merry jape to see my worthy father foot it yarely in the air of a sudden like a feat'though portly-gazelle."

Philip' sighed with relief. "What you want is a firecracker. I'm sure I can make you one. Wonder where Dorothea keeps her gunpowder. She must have some—I'm sure no home on this plane of existence is without it."

He peered up into the shadows over the mantelpiece, where three canisters stood in a row . . . but they were clearly marked *Mercury, Sulphur, Salt*. No gunpowder.

"Or, given the ingredients," he went on, opening one of the cabinets in the wall and looking dubiously into its cluttered interior, "I think I could make the gunpowder. After all, I *am* a scientist."

The boy made a derisive noise, which Philip[2] pretended to ignore.

"I'll need potassium nitrate to start with," he went on, prodding a tangled mass of roots with a gingerly finger, "or, as you'd probably call it, saltpeter . . . *Ouch!*"

Something inside the cupboard had bitten his finger sharply. He slammed the door shut and leaned against it, although, now that he had time to consider the brief glimpse he'd had of his assailant, he fancied it was only a bat. He must speak to Dorothea about tidying up the place. There was such a thing as a room looking too lived-in.

Miraculously, he found the compound he sought on trial of a musty cobwebbed jar that lurked at the back of the shelves. There was sulphur in ample quantities at hand and he managed to procure some charcoal from the fireplace. The boy eyed him skeptically as he mixed the explosive, taking time out now and again to nurse his bitten finger.

"'Tseems an oddly roundabout way to produce the jape I crave," the youngster said as Philip^2 poured his mixture into an improvised cylinder of stiff paper and set about contriving a fuse.

"Methinks it might prove more perilous than I fancy."

"Don't worry—it will do the trick," said Philip^2. He made a second smaller firecracker with the remainder of his mixture, noted that Perkin sat crouched, with his ears back, beneath a bench in the far corner. The big cat looked as if it wished it could get through the wall.

"There," said Philip^2 with pardonable pride. "We'll test the smaller cracker Just to make sure."

He put it on the hearth, plucked a brand from the fire and lighted the brief fuse.

There was a brief flare of bright light as the powder caught—then a sharp sucking sound and the firecracker vanished abruptly and without visible cause—or visible remains. Philip^2 blinked and uttered a very ancient Anglo-Saxon word.

"'Tis my belief," said the boy suspiciously, "that you're an imposter. For, weak in the mazard though he might be, Dorothea's spouse would ken where the stores were kept, 'less he were clean bestraught."

"Nonsense!" Philip^2 snapped, hastily righting a retort which he had knocked over, before the snake inside could escape. It was annoying that the child should be so much more perceptive than his own wife—than the other Philip's own wife, rather. Philip^2 unstoppered a bottle and smelled it. Could it really be wine?

He saw the boy regarding him and hastily replaced the cork. "Nonsense!" he repeated. "It's just that she keeps changing everything around so, I can't find a . . . *Dolly!*" he exclaimed enthusiastically. "Am *I* glad to see you!"

For the sorceress had just reappeared in the room. "I was halfway to Lady Alison's," she explained breathlessly, brushing back her ruddy locks, "when I minded me that you were something addled—something informal I mean—Philip."

"*Addled* is the proper term," commented the child. "I wot well who has the wit in this household."

"—and might, being a thought humorous, bodge the trade," she continued, ignoring him. "I myself must have had a touch of the lunes to leave you without forewarning. Therefore, I say to you now—would y'not essay any contrivance today, but merely content yourself with inscribing all orders upon this tablet, and I'll fulfill 'em from the scrippage. You *can* write, can't you?"

"Of course I can! And what's more, I could fill the orders, too, if I knew where everything was kep!. All this kid needs is a firecracker.

Now if I had some gunpowder, I could—"

"*Gunpowder!*'" she cried. "You're mazed, Philip. Gunpowder in the Twentieth Century!

There've been no guns extant since the Eighteenth, for a spell ne'er fails to find its mark, while guns are monstrous uncertain engines. Is't an explosion you want, princox?" she addressed the child. "I ha' the very thing."

Reaching into a cabinet, she pulled out a paper packet. Nothing bit *her*, Philip[2] observed resentfully. She must have had the contents of her cupboards well trained.

"When y'wish to create a rare hurley," she said to the boy, "but asperse the powder in the air while reciting the words charactered upon the parchment. The result will exceed your most extensive aspirations. "

"And the price?" the boy asked suspiciously. "I warn you, sorceress, maugre my youth, I'm not one to be gulled."

"Three ducats," replied Dorothe. "A small price for so large an explosion."

"It seems just," the child admitted, counting three pieces of gold into her palm. "But I'll be back should it rail in its effect!" " Oh, you' ll not be back, skipper!" Dorothea told him. "I'll warrant you that!"

The boy disappeared.

Perkin came and rubbed against Philip^{2}s legs. Dorothea, regarding the animal affectionately, threw it a morsel of mummy. She seemed pleased that it liked Philip^2. Philip^2 wondered whether Philip^1 had used the cat brutally. If so, he would make up for it. Reaching down, he tickled Perkin's ear. Perkin purred. Dorothea looked at both fondly.

"By the way," Philip^2 asked, straightening, "what was in the package you gave the kid?"

"Oh, a trick, naught more," Dorothea replied carelessly, dragging a snaggle-toothed gold comb through her tangled hair, with small effect. "Merely a quaint contrivance for cleaving th'atom."

"Cleaving-splitting the atom'" Philip^2 yelled. "That's impossible. It would blow him up and his house and his family and—and . . ."

"And all else for miles about," Dorothea agreed cheerfully. "If his family is caught with its spells down. But he dwells a goodly distance from here, for I recognized the lad, cunningly though the little estridge thought he'd altered himself. Did he think he could blear my eyes?" She snorted. "'Tis the little crown prince and we stand sore in need of a new regime if his parents wax careless,"

"But how does it *work?*" Philip^2 demanded. After all, an abstract scientist should steer clear of politics—he was interested in the principles involved. "You can't split the atom without deuterium, uranium and so forth. A whole fission pile, as a matter of fact."

"What manner of spell is that?"

"It's not a *spell!* It's a—well, a factory, so to speak."

Dorothea smiled contemptuously. "Cleaving an atom needs no manufactory, sweet fool. All that's required is the proper enchantment."

"But—but you've got to have the proper equipment to split the atom," he protested. It stands to reason."

"Prove it then," she suggested, logically enough, he was forced to admit.

"I haven't an Oak Ridge on me. My God, woman, it's a *huge* plant!"

"Make one then."

"But I *can't*—it takes a lot of time and money and skilled technicians . . ."

"The spell," she retorted, "costs but three ducats and takes but a moment. Even if your 'science' works, as mayhap it does, for I'm not parochial enough to think my system of magic th' only one extant—'tis only the best—it could not be as speedy and economical as my spell."

He did not ask her for a demonstration because, although he knew it *couldn't* be, he had a sinister suspicion that perhaps it *would,* and he didn't precisely care to be caught in the middle of an atomic explosion.

"Why should it work?" he demanded.

"Why shouldn't it?" she replied practically.

"A spell can't work. Now take science. I perform an experiment, go through the same procedures and the results are always the same, providing I haven't made any error. For instance, at a certain altitude, if I heat water to a certain degree, it will always boil. You must know what I mean," he insisted. "You have a fire under your pot."

She grinned. "'Tis but for decorative effect, my innocent. Ha' you ne'er heard of a fire used solely for ornament?"

"Sure, but if it boils water, it's not just ornamental."

"Mark me well." She moved her hands in an intricate pattern.

"Round about,

Low and high,

Flames go out;

Fire die."

The room was now absolutely dark except for the glow of two pairs of eyes—the green ones of the cat, the yellow ones of Dorothea.

"I forgot," her voice came hollow in the blackness, "you cannot see in the dark.

Aroint thee, night;

Away with gloom!

Let truth's own light

Illume this room."

And the chamber was filled with a strange blue radiance which, although it illuminated more than the firelight had—perhaps *because* it illuminated more—gave a particularly horrid aspect to the room.

Now he saw the steel-strong spiderwebs that stretched from beam to beam, their round-bodied occupants watching him impersonally with flat yellow eyes like Dorothea's. He saw that the raven perched over the doorway was *not* stuffed. He saw clearly the subjects of the smoke-dimmed tapestries and hastily looked away.

"You'll allow the firelight is more friendly-seeming," Dorothea smiled. There was not much attractive about her smile now. Under the blue, almost fluorescent light, her skin took on a pallid purplish tinge and her elf-locks seemed to curl into writhing snakes with tiny jewel eyes that stared at him. "Look into the cauldron, knave. See, 'tis empty. Now I fill it with water."

And the pot, whose black iron bottom he had just seen bare and dry was filled to the brim with clear liquid.

Philip[2], teeth were chattering, but he still strove for reason and logic. "H—how do I know it's water?"

She frowned, and he involuntarily retreated a step. "Take my word for it, man! Moreover, any liquid—whatever it be—needs heat to boil, does it not?"

He nodded.

She pointed a long finger at the iron vessel.

"Double, double, no toil, no trouble

No fire . . . to make *my* cauldron bubble."

The water—liquid or whatever it was—definitely was boiling, and boiling violently. And the pot hung over cold ashes and emptiness. There was no fire.

Dorothea's voice sounded very remote in his ears. "Shall I restore the flames, sweet chuck? Meseems they are more cozy than this light."

Again he nodded without speaking. He was more frightened than he had been even when he first found himself in this place. And he was cold inside and thought maybe he was going to be sick.

How could there be such a place as this, where everything was contrary to the principles on which his whole life was based? He knew it couldn't exist—that it was mere fancy and yet . . . here he was. And he wasn't mad—madness would have been a relief he was clearly, horribly sane. Even if he could return to his own plane of existence now, the only way he could do it would be by employing the methods of this world: by using a spell.

And what good would that be? It would forever haunt him. As a scientist, he could not deny to himself that this place would continue to exist and mock everything he stood for. Knowing that, he could no longer be content with the science of his own world. Yet there was no place for him in this one. Wherever he went now, he was lost.

There was only one thing he could do—adapt the workably scientific principles of his native plane to the necromantic laws which appeared to prevail in this one. Already he was beginning to understand that his firecracker had failed to work because of a universal centuries-old spell banning the use of gunpowder.

And therein lay the key, Philip[2] decided. On his original plane, the powers of the mind in general were ineffective against the powers of the machine. On this strange world in which he found himself, the reverse seemed to apply.

Why? What lay beneath this about-face of so-called natural laws? And what were its applications? Philip[2] felt a challenge that was worthy of his talent, perhaps even beyond it. But surely here was the perfect field assignment for a hitherto humdrum man of science. Here was a whole new world to explore, to study, to test, to understand.

And here was Dorothea, with her weird but very definite charm . . . what's more, with what began to look like a definite attraction to himself.

He looked at the large and useless firecracker and then closed his eyes, hearing Dorothea's eerie voice chant,

"Black is white.

Left is right.

Lower will be higher.

Out true light.

Go, clear sight.

Flare up, magic fire."

He heard the crackling of flames.

"Open your eyes, sweet. The fire burns again. All is well—there's naught to fear."

He felt warmth on his face and when he ventured to open his eyes, the blue light was gone, the fire burned under the cauldron and Dorothea was merely a fashionably thin red-haired woman . . . no longer a snaky-haired enchantress.

She smiled at him and he knew whatever was or was not, he could never return to his own world.

It wasn't until after she had gone that he remembered she had asked him whether he could write. No matter how little a wife may know her own husband, she'd know whether he could write or not. Of course! She wouldn't have explained the difference between the two planes to her *husband*. She knew who Philip[2] was, where he had come from, probably where he was going. She knew everything. What a devil of a woman to be in love with!

He pulled the cork out of the bottle whose contents had smelled like wine and recklessly drank whatever the fluid was. Nothing that happened to him from then on mattered.

V

Philip[1] absent-mindedly enchanted the front door and it opened afore he bethought himself that 'twould have been more seemly to use the key with which Dora had provided him. Previously it had seemed a thought strange to him that doors and windows were in ordinary use here. Now he knew the reason—there was so little magic in this world that it must be conserved for deeds of import.

How even a third-rank wizard (for he must admit that he was held in insufficient esteem on his own plane) could have festinately mastered this realm! Or so it seemed. But such was not to be the case! He had bodged this existence, as he had bodged his former one.

Mayhap Dorothea was right—he was a sad drumbler and a fool's fool in any realm. And now he was trapped indeed, having performed something so horrendous here that he could not quite brain its significance . . . and yet unable to return to his own, having been witless enough to lose the phylactery somewhere.

Perhaps, and he'd been hopeful for a moment, the same ingredients could be assembled in this existence—but no, even were it possible, 'twould take too long. "Oh, Dolly, Dolly!" he groaned inwardly. "If y'do not haste to fetch me, I'm like to perish most miserably."

But he had glimpsed her in his crystal ball a-kissing and a-hugging of the other Philip, whom he had so cunningly disguised with his magical arts that she *must* think him her own spouse—'twas the only reasonable explanation. But it gave him small comfort to think that he was like to die for being a good wizard rather than for being a bad one.

"Od's pittikins!" he moaned. "They'll stretch me on the rack or belike break me on the wheel—neither of which strikes me as an agreeable end to all my charms."

At the sound of his cough, for he had indeed taken a bisson rheum in this benighted clime, the homely clattering of dishes ceased and Dora pattered out on delightful stilt heels.

"What's the matter, sweetie pie?" she asked, turning up her painted plum-cheeked face to be bussed. It would break his heart to part from her, though less if the parting were to result from enchantment rather than death. "Did something go wrong?"

"Aye, there has been something of a coil, dearest chuck," he said wearily, hurling his headgear upon a table. "It appears that th'orgulous yarlets who seem to hold the power of the high, the low and the middle justice over me do not fancy my pedagogic method."

"But why?" Her purblind eyes stared. "You're teaching the kids just the same way you always did, aren't you, lambchop?" She tightened her arms about him. *"Aren't you?"*

He could not unfold the whole matter to the wench without discovering to her that he was not her true husband. Had he any hope of an incontinent return to his own realm, the truth needs must out forthwith, however. And what a pretty garboil Philip[2] would have found upon his return—a just merit for having treated his lovesome wife so scurvily. But the bag was lost and with it hope was lost as well.

"I ha' varied my methods, my love," he said cautiously. "I've developed a new doctrine which effects the same results as the logger-headed procedures which the flap-eared measles term as 'scientific method.' 'Scientific method,' push! Certes, but y'have a ponderous and ineffectual system of magical arts here under the name of 'science.'"

She stared at him blankly. He dragged himself wearily into the principal chamber and threw himself upon the couch.

"Marry," he sighed, "I'm fatigate."

CALL ME WIZARD

Dora unfastened the moist apron that was the sweet badge of her subservience and sat on the arm of the couch, stroking his hair. Her hazel eyes were troubled.

"But what happened, Phil?" she asked. "Did they—did they fire you? I hoped they'd let you stay until your contract expired."

"There was a pother when I but 'tempted to teach my class an exceeding simple spell. A child in my own—why, a babe in arms should know't! And a mage of some apparent dignity, who had been a-spying on my pedagogy, conducted me to a private apartment where he and divers other learned gentlemen broached a foison of witless queries."

"W—who do you mean?"

"A pathetical sway-backed antick who termed himself 'the head of the department.' He then desired that I return to my own quarters t'attend his pleasure."

"You mean *Professor Brunschweiger* asked you to go home?"

Dora's soft visage quivered and she burst into tears. A fluxive wench, in truth, but she wept right prettily. "It's the end, Philip. You'll be fired and you'll never get another job on a campus. We'll starve."

"Be of good cheer, beloved," he consolated, drawing her fubsy form down to his side. "For with you t'inspire me, I am certain sure that in some other employment I may make a more efficacious use of my skills."

The future was not so dark then. Nay, if all that could happen was that he'd be expulsed from his post, why, 'twould be a rare good thing. He would set up as wizard ordinary and thrive in this fond world. The loss of his receipt did not matter so much, although he'd prefer to have it to hand should he be imperiled again. Natheless, 'twas a relief to hear he'd not be broken on the wheel—he had not fancied the idea at all.

"But you can't do anything else but teach, honey," Dora objected. "You keep complaining about that all the time. Philip, sometimes you almost seem like a different man entirely."

"I *am* a different man, dearest chuck," be said, putting his arms about her. "Believe me."

She smiled at him. "I do, Philip. Truly I do."

*

He had forgotten to ask Dorothea how to get out of the. room, Philip' disgruntedly realized. But then, since she obviously knew he was not her husband, she probably wanted to keep him there.

Not that he blamed her really, he thought, observing his reflection in the watery depths of a gilt-framed mirror.

"Mirror, mirror on the wall," he said. "Who is the handsomest man of all?" He waited expectantly, but the mirror proved to be a very ordinary mirror, after all, and made no reply.

He wondered how he'd look in the costume of this world. Not bad, be decided!

And Dolly was a good-looking girl too, with, as far as be could judge from that flour sack she kept wearing, an excellent figure. If only she'd take care of her appearance. Perhaps he could show her how before he was snatched back.

He looked regretfully at the empty bottle that had contained, if not wine, then a remarkably good imitation. If he were a magician, he could probably conjure up more . . . or maybe even Scotch. He wondered idly how difficult it was to learn wizardry, just supposing that, for some reason or other, he'd be forced to stay on this plane.

One wall of the room was shelved, and held row upon row of books. Perhaps he'd find something useful among them. He peered at the faded gilt lettering on the backs. It was hard to read in such a dim light. The bottom shelf seemed to hold what he wanted: *Elementary Thaumaturgy, First Steps in Sorcery, A Primer of Necromancy.*

Philip[2] wondered with a trace of envy what it must be like to be trained from childhood in the foundations of magic. He reminded himself that, as a man of science, he could not admit the existence of anything so illogical as magic . . . what he meant actually was the new set of factual conditions and causes to which he was going to have to become accustomed.

And he knew, emotionally as well as mentally, that he dreaded returning to his somber and sterile life as a physics instructor back on his native plane. He felt an unpleasant little chill of embarrassment—of loathing—at the thought of awakening in the middle of the night and finding Dora, rather than Dorothea, lying beside him in the Swedish modern bed.

He made up his mind that he was going to do everything possible to ensure that Dorothea should not tire of him before he mastered enough necromancy to protect himself. For he knew that in his wife—or rather in his alter-ego's wife—lay his sole protection for the present against the incantations of a spell-run world.

He opened *First Steps in Sorcery*. In faded handwriting on the flyleaf was written: "To Dorothea on her eighth birthday, from her loving Aunt Hecate, October 31, 1929." And underneath, in a childish scrawl:

"He who dares this book to borrow Shall be a toad upon the morrow.

Dear Dorothea—how glad he was that he had not known her as a child!

It was not the intricate lettering and obscure phraseology alone, he was forced to admit to himself, that made the spells incomprehensible to him. He had almost given up when he found one that looked simple. He tried it.

"Hocus pocus," he said, "here's a crocus."

Nothing happened.

"I might have known," he sighed. "You've got to be born to this sort of thing."

And then he looked more carefully at the text. There was a magic sign to go with it. He moved his fingers carefully. "Hocus pocus, here's a crocus."

And there was a small white crocus in his hand.

He stood looking at the flower, which was undersized and anemic, but undoubtedly genuine. "I did it myself! Look, Perkin!"

The cat rubbed his head against Philip^{2}s knee and purred approvingly. "Hocus pocus," Philip^2 repeated, "here's another crocus."

And there was a big yellow one!

Perkin miaued loudly.

*

"Meseems y'are a flower fancier, good sir," said a dulcet voice, "for, certes, never in this life have I seen so many croci."

Philip^2 turned and the lady smiled at him. She was tall and slender, with long green eyes and long golden hair parted in the center of a broad white brow and drawn smoothly back in a knot behind her small head. Her robes had been designed by a descendant of the original Peeping Tom, evidently, and what they revealed was damned good.

Cosmetics, he noted, were not unknown on this plane of existence. Apparently Dorothea was one of those intellectual women who disdained all adornment. Or perhaps she worked so hard that she had no time to make herself beautiful. Poor girl, she did rush about while that good-for-nothing husband of hers had probably taken it easy.

He looked at the lady more carefully. There were emeralds in her ears and clasped around the slender neck, enhancing the white shoulders and bosom that rose out of the tight-fitting black gown. She must have money, he thought appraisingly.

Her voice was low and musical. "I seek the Lady Dorothea. She was to have attended me at my bedside this forenoon, but she came not, so, being anxious for her services, I came myself despite my malady."

"You must be Lady Alison," Philip[2] said, smiling. "She just left for your place. You must have passed each other in—whatever it is you come through. But why should *you* need a love-potion?"

"Alas, all men have not the same tastes," she sighed. "Just as all women do not. Now Dorothea has oft described you as a monstrous ill-favored and corky rogue—"

The other Philip must have been a good deal different in appearance from him, Philip[2] decided, even though they were the same man. Strange, how much environment could affect appearance.

"—Whereas y'are a proper and most courteous gentleman." Alison adjusted her hair with delicate white fingers on which more emeralds sparkled. "Could not *you* brew me the potion, good sir? I understand y'are also a sorcerer of parts,"

She was flattering him, he knew, for Dorothea would never have described her husband's abilities so favorably. And he was enjoying her flattery. However, much as he longed to impress the girl, there was no use in his meddling around with wizardry—unless she wanted a crocus, which seemed unlikely.

"I'm afraid I don't know how to brew a potion," he confessed. "If you'll give me your name and address, I'll write them down and tell

Dorothea you called. She'll be sorry to have missed you." That was a good touch, he thought. He was picking up the business fast.

"Don't know *how?*" she repeated, her glaucous eyes widening. "You mean y'admit that y'have no skill in sorcery?"

He stared back at her defiantly. "Well, if I can't do that kind of work, what's the use of making a fool of myself by pretending I can!"

Probably he was spoiling Philip[1]'s reputation, but it served the guy right for switching planes and sending Philip[2] to one where he was of even less account than his own. Still, if he could conjure up crocuses, he could probably go on to more advanced spells under Dorothea's loving guidance.

Suddenly a horrid thought struck him. What if Philip[1] came back and insisted on assuming his old place and his—former wife? What could he—Philip[2]—do to stop the other? And then he took comfort. He might not know what to do, but Dorothea would. She'd take care of him. She'd take care of the other Philip, too, if he dared to stick his ugly nose back in this world! Women like Dorothea, he decided, had many uses beyond the kitchen and the bedchamber.

Alison was speaking ". . . I ne'er thought I'd see the day when a man'd willingly accept the fact that the male is not the female's equal for wit and wizardry."

She moved closer to him. He liked her perfume; it was heavy and sensuous—he must buy Dolly a bottle of the same, if she'd lend him the money .

"By my troth, y'not only have a seemly assemblance, but are a modest and soft-spoken fellow into the bargain. I like you well and if it so happens that y'are not indifferent to me, we'll need no magical arts or love potions . . . for the cad for whom I destined the brew was, although well-enough favored, a very coistrel like my own forked lord—who is, moreover, foul to boot."

"Really, madam!" Philip[2] took a step backward. After all, he *was* married to Dorothea—as far as Alison knew, anyhow. Although, from what she'd said, it seemed as though Alison also were married, so you could hardly expect her to show much respect for other people's legal ties. He was still too unsure of himself to beg for trouble on this alien plane.

"Be not strange with me, sweet necromancer," she breathed huskily, advancing upon him. "A little backwardness is admirable in the man, but not when 'tis carried too far. Once I spurned a youth who, though beautiful as the sun, blushed and shrank overmuch. Shortly afterward the poor knave died of a decline. Take warning by this." Philip[2] retreated further. He had never objected to a little harmless flirtation—only Dora had—but the flirtation he saw in this predatory female's eye as she reached out for him did not impress him as harmless.

Flight would be unmanly . . . besides, where could he flee? He wished Dorothea would return. He, a male, needing protection from a woman! But then he was a stranger, lost in a strange world. And Lady Alison was both attractive and dangerous.

There was a hissing sound. Perkin thrust himself between Alison and Philip[2], his green eyes blazing defiance, his back arched into a hoop as he spat at her.

"I see you're not entirely without protection," Alison said smoothly. "Dorothea, I apprehend, was not so casual, after all. Still, my bent is great and so I am minded to test th'extent of the cat's powers."

She came on. Philip[2] was afraid something terrible was going to happen, for Perkin was growling and swelling up like a furry balloon. He did not so much care if Alison came to harm, but he looked upon the cat as a friend. Yet all he could do himself was hiccup faintly. The wine must have been enchanted.

Alison looked at him and her shining eyes seemed to grow to three times their former size. "You must come out of this house with me. The spell is too powerful here. *Come!*"

"I—I can't," he said. I don't know how."

"Move your fingers in this wise!" she commanded. Do it, knave, *do it! And do it rightly!*"

He obeyed, partly because he wanted to know the spell and partly because he was afraid of her. He repeated after her the mystic chant,

"Neutron, deuteron, positron, proton,

Blessed or diabolic, you'll

Spread apart each molecule;

While we are in *transitu*,

The atoms part to let us through,

So we pass through walls or doors,

Windows, ceilings, halls and floors:

Neutron, deuteron, positron, proton . . . "

And he found himself out in the street. There were houses ranged on both sides—rows of semi-detached houses all exactly similar in style just like those of his own Dulcamara Drive. Only the architecture was different and he found it, in the cold blue light that poured down from a strange sky, singularly unpleasant. It was charming to have gargoyles as water spouts, but he didn't like the way they were watching him. Dorothea had been right in keeping him inside.

Why had he ever let this woman lure him out into the street—this woman who, for all of her beauty . . . if you could call anyone beautiful who had golden snakes for hair and tied the poor little things in a knot. He could call the SPCA—they might help the snakes if not him. But there probably was no SPCA here. People here were most likely cruel to animals. Animals!

"*Perkin!*" he called. "Perkin, save me!"

55

CALL ME WIZARD

A miau of anguish came from inside the house—but no cat.

Alison smiled. "He cannot leave the house, for Dorothea has so devised it. Why think you I led you out on the street, sweet geck? But fear not, I shall do you no hurt s'long as you serve my purpose."

There was nobody to help him. And Lady Alison was coming toward him purposefully again. What was he to do?

VI

A bell shrilled. Philip[1] leaped from his seat.

Dora smiled wanly. "You're all on edge, dear. That's just the door. It must be Brunschweiger." She lifted the front window cloth slightly and peered out. Use of his crystal would have been less cumbersome, but he could hardly suggest it to her. "Yes, it is—and there's somebody else with him. It must be a man from the FBI or something."

She turned and faced him, breathing heavily. "Philip, they mustn't see you!"

"Whatever you will, my love," Philip[1] subscribed, and made himself invisible afore he bethought himself of what he was doing.

She gave a faint shriek and clapped her band across her mouth. "Ph—Philip!"

He reappeared again. "Sorry, my love, a temporary aberration." But no madness could extenuate *this*, he knew.

She gripped him by the shoulders. "Philip—or whatever your name is—I know you aren't my husband. I don't care *who* you are. But *what* are you?"

The bell pealed again—tolled rather, Philip[1] thought, straightening the lapels of his upper garment.

"No time t'unfold the matter now, sweet," he said, patting her hand. 'Fore God, he loved this dame a—life. "First I must front these good gentlemen."

"Do you think you can get away with it?" she asked. "It's the way you talk, mostly—not a foreign accent, but—but like an actor or something."

"Rest you easy, gracious lady," be consoled. "I've already affronted the professor and he does not doubt that I'm your spouse; Belike he

57

fancies I'm bestraught! In any case, I needs must face them, be it soon or late."

"Aye," she said dully. "Oh, Lord; I'm beginning to talk like you! That's wrong—you've got to learn to talk like me!"

"Of a certainty," he agreed. "And as soon as I have dealt with these snipes, you shall apply yourself to my tutelage in your charming dialect."

The bell rang again.

She clutched his arm. "He'll be angry at being kept waiting," she said. "Maybe we should pretend we're not home."

He thrust her aside gently. "Nay, love, ours must be the bold face if we're to—as you most aptly remarked—'get away with it.'"

She looked at him with a respect and worship he had never seen in Dorothea's eyes. "Now I'm sure you're not my husband," she breathed.

Professor Brunschweiger, a large, paunchy varlet, wearing barnacles attached to a black rib—and, stood on the doorstep. With him was another knave whom Philip! had not yet encountered—a fellow younger and ruddier of face.

"I give you good—den, gentles," Philip! said heartily. "Certes, I could ha' wished for no better company to disturb my afternoon's rest."

He expected his superior to be as wroth as he had been the previous day, but Professor Brunscbweiger's voice was surprisingly mild as he whispered to his companion,

"He's been talking like this for the last couple of days."

The other spread his hands wide. "The vagaries of genius," he sighed. "I've had to deal with so much of it, Professor."

Dora peered at him from under Philip's arm. "Who are you?"

"Dr. McIntosh," Professor Brunschweiger said with gentle reproach, "is a representative of the United States Government."

"The FBI!" Dora wailed. "I knew it; I knew it!"

Philip[1] trembled. Apparently it meant the Iron Maiden, after all!

Brunschweiger and McIntosh looked at one another. "Seems to be catching," the professor said. "May we come in, Mrs. Gardner?"

Dora and Philip[1] stepped back silently to permit them to come in.

"But what ha' I done?" Philip[1] burst forth suddenly. "What's amiss? I swear I had no baleful intent, whate'er 'twas I did."

"Sometimes I wonder," Professor Brunschweiger told the government man, "how much of his aberration stems from a breakdown and how much from a distorted sense of humor. You know what be was doing—the class asked him bow the anti-gravity unit worked and he was actually teaching them a spell. A *spell*, mind you! And the little fools were swallowing it. I don't know what the younger generation is corning to."

Dr. McIntosh laughed heartily. 'Twas apparent he thought whatever Philip[1] had done to be of a merry nature.

Philip[1] gave a weak laugh. "I must avow I am a gamesome rogue," he confessed.

"But why didn't you confide In me, Philip?" Professor Brunschweiger asked with sorrow. "If I hadn't dropped in to observe your class at just that moment, I might never have known . . . The reason I was sitting in on the class," he explained to Dr. Mcintosh, "was that we're thinking of recommending Dr. Gardner for an assistant professorship."

There was a loud gasp from Dora.

"An assistant professorship, of course," Dr. McIntosh agreed." And no more than he's entitled to, from what I hear. I imagine he wanted to, surprise you, Professor Brunschweiger. And also—he probably wanted to test the—the device—in front of the students to make sure it wouldn't blow up. Isn't that so, Dr. Gardner?"

"I could not have phrased it better myself," Philip[1] agreed with him, amiably enough.

"Now, sir," Dr. McIntosh said, declining his person forward, "I might as well be frank about my reason for coming here. As soon as he saw your demonstration, Professor Brunschweiger telephoned Washington and they got in touch with me immediately. I'm their field representative working in this vicinity. The government, Dr. Gardner, as you may have guessed, is interested in the anti-gravity unit which you have developed."

"One of *our* instructors," Professor' Brunschweiger crooned. "One of *my* professors! It'll make the school!"

"Will it also make Philip?" Dora inquired.

Dr. McIntosh smiled. "He's already made. Wait until you see the afternoon paper! . . . Dr. Gardner, I would like to see a demonstration of your anti-gravity machine. If it works—and I'm sure I can take Professor Brunschweiger's word for it, only I must see it myself—the government is prepared to negotiate generously. Between military and industrial use, it will mean millions for you."

"Millions . . ." Philip[1] repeated thoughtfully.

"Millions!" Dora cried. *"Millions!* Oh, Philip, *darling!"*

Whatever the millions were in, he reflected, they must be valuable for Dora to grow so avid. Let the momes have the formula . . . but 'twould be of no avail to teach their government the spell, for they'd not credit such a thing. Still, given time, he could fashion some device that would have the semblance of an engine, yet contain the spell within it.

His pensive eye fell upon the phonograph. The very thing—although he'd have to alter its outward seeming somewhat so that it should not be known for what it was. "The device has gone a trifle awry since I last made use of it," he explained. Being a tricksy rogue, he could outwit anyone in this innocent realm. "Were you to return on the morrow, I should be right glad t'unfold to you the result of my clever conclusions."

"Tomorrow it is," agreed Dr. McIntosh enthusiastically. Everybody shook hands all around once more. "Mrs. Gardner," the government fellow said, "you have a great man for a husband!"

Dora put her arm through Philip[1]'s and squeezed it amorously.

"I know," she breathed.

"Oh, push!" Philip' said modestly.

*

There was a shriek: "Ho, housewife!" And Dorothea stood in the middle of the street, her cloak still swirling with the sudden cessation of movement, her hair in wilder disorder than ever, her bosom heaving with breathlessness and fury. "So, foul jade! Make love to my own charitable lord, would you, th'instant my back is turned! Fitchew!"

Alison was as calm as if nothing out of the way had happened. "Y'came not to me in time, good chewet," she shrugged, "so I did graciously dispatch myself to your abode. How was I to know y'had already set forth? And who's to blame me for seeking some solacement? I could scarce have whiled away the time of waiting by conversation with your spouse, for, as you've so oft observed yourself, he's as witless as a cucumber."

Just see how smart you'd be if you were suddenly stuck in a strange universe, Philip[2] thought venomously.

"Giglet!" Dorothea spat. "Can y'not clap eyes upon a fair man—or for that matter a foul one, for you're marvelous indiscriminate—without trying your liberal arts upon him? Well 'twas y'could not pass th'entrance examinations to the School of Sorcery. Had you sufficient skill to brew your own potions, by my troth, there's not a man in America but who'd have been in your chamber by now!"

"Dolly!" Philip[2] protested. "You shouldn't talk like that! To a customer especially!"

Dorothea gave vent to derisive laughter. "Customer, aye, you have the right word for her, sweet knave. A customer she is indeed! Come lip me for that, peat!"

She kissed him soundly. "Let us within the house—it's mortal cold out here."

And they were back in the warm, relaxing firelight. Perkin pattered forth to greet them with a miau of relief.

"He did his best, Dolly," Philip[2] said as the sorceress was about to reproach the cat. "He really did."

Perkin rubbed his velvety head against Philip[2]'s hand.

"Aye, he did his best, Dolly," Alison sneered. "But a cat, after all, though he be no worse than a man, is no better either."

"What!" Dorothea cried. "You dare to follow me back into the house, strumpet, after your shameless behavior?"

Alison shrugged. "I need no defense, sorceress, for well you know that I'm a dame of strong affections. Y'should have come festinately with the potion. And you should not have let so lovesome a fellow out of your sight—he's so natural, I wonder that half the female livers in town have not been set afire by his modest habit. Or have y'kept him mewed up like a sheep?" She gave a metallic laugh. "Aye, I can see by your face that y'have. Doll, you lack proper assurance to be possess't of such a man."

So Dorothea had not kept him locked up to keep him from getting out, but to keep other women from getting in. Or, rather, from discovering that she had such a prize as he—for there was no keeping anyone out in this universe. Dear little woman—he hiccuped again—she thought only of his welfare. Not like Dora, who cared only for herself.

Alison continued airily: "Sith I observe I shall get nowhere with your spouse—although, had you not arrived so incontinently, there might have been another tale to tell—will y'not concoct me a mess of th'amorous drug, sweet charmer, so that I may fascinate another?"

Dorothea snorted. "How d'ye ken I'll not put hebenon in't?"

"Because the whole world knows I purchase my charms from you," Alison yawned. "Did they think you to have slain me a-purpose, 'twould be immoment, but they'd be certain sure you'd put the poison in by misprision. Would y'wish to be known as a slubberly sorceress?"

Dorothea grunted.

"I'm your best client, Doll," Alison went on. "Don't forget, such conquests as I have effected without the aid of magical arts—and they have been notable ones, perdy!—ha' been ascribed to your mysteries. If y'poison me, you poison your own best advertisement. And all for the sake of such a trumpery thing as a man. Fie, Doll, you're too tricksy a dame to do a fond thing like that."

"Y'have the right on't," Dorothea agreed, moodily opening various cupboard doors and flinging ingredients into the pot. "However, henceforth do not call upon me here at my abode. If y'have need of me, send for me. I'll not have my husband jaded by your irregulous suggestions."

"As y'will, good sorceress," Alison said, slanting her long green eyes provocatively at Philip[2]. He lowered his. "And now the potion. Pray he expedient, for I am fancy-sick, though I care not overmuch whom I fancy."

Dorothea waved her hand over the cauldron.

"Take werewolf's eyes,
The wings of flies,
A mandrake root,
And then add to 't
The liver of a dove,
A griffin's bone,
A hollow groan,
A corpse's feet,
And it's complete—
The elixir of love."

There was a flash of blue flame from the pot. Dorothea dipped her ladle into the brew, which had a most unaphrodisiac odor. In fact, Philip[2] thought, he seemed to have smelled the same thing somewhere before, and very recently, too. She filled a small vial with its smoking contents.

"Mind you, lady," she said as she handed the bottle to Alison, "make yourself a stranger to my spouse or I'll not guarantee that my emotions will fordo my business acumen."

"He's a goodly fellow," Alison said, handing Dorothea three ducats, which seemed to be a standard fee. Socialized sorcery, probably. "Yet there are other men as goodly. But there's no sorceress can brew a love potion as cleverly as you, Doll."

She blew a kiss at Philip[2]. "Now you know the way out of this house, pray visit me when y'can escape your mistress's eye. I dwell at 1313 Verbena Avenue and the latch-string will always be out for you, charitable rogue."

And, before Dorothea could utter a word of protest, she vanished.

"Dame Alison takes on as if the potion were destined for the man," Dorothea remarked, "although she needs not such at all, being a well-favored woman, although in a fashion I myself, were I a man, would not admire."

She looked an anxious question at Philip[2].

"Oh, I don't think she's anything so special," he said. "It's the clothes and the paint. If you fixed yourself up like that, Doll, you'd look a thousand times better than her."

"D'ye think so?" She turned to look at her reflection in the mirror. "Y'may have the right of it, at that" Then she sighed. "Marry, but I'm clean forspent!" She sank into a chair. "Would you be good enough, love, to store my gabardine? Sooth t'say, I have not the strength for so simple a task."

Philip[2] obediently hung her cloak in the wardrobe. He realized that, though she had couched it as a request, it was a Command and if he stayed in this place, he would have to continue following her orders. Unless he could get his own science to work properly . . .

She sighed and relaxed into the depths of the chair. "The potion Alison desires is rather to revive her own flagging energies, for she can conceive of no other pursuit in life save that of the opposing sex. But y'made stout resistance, Philip," she went on, "and I could not altogether ha' blamed you, had you complied with her riggish purposes—specially since you were fuddled wi' my best Madeira, for I winded your breath, rogue, when I bussed you. Wenches like her, with wealth and leisure at their fingertips, have more time t'give to the blandishing of men than the knaves' hard-working spouses."

"Dorothea," Philip[2] said, lurching slightly, "you know perfectly well that I am *not* your husband. I should have realized from the start that a sorceress like you would have known right away. The trouble is, I don't believe in sorcery. The whole thing's—it's illogical."

"But our logic is not your logic, fond knave," Dorothea said in a voice that was unexpectedly tender. "Just as yours would seem irrational to us. I thought you'd ha' brained that by now. Truth to tell, I did think y'were my own Philip at the start, for you're marvelous like him. And though I knew he purposed to visit another realm, to be open about it I ne'er thought he'd succeed. The varlet had more doctrine than I allowed."

"You knew about the other—place then?" he asked, incredulous.

"For sure I did. Did I not tell you that you—that is, your counterpart—chanced upon the spell in an old tome? Who d'ye think left the book lying about for him to chance upon? No, I was awearied of the valanced snipe, yet for the sake of th'affection in which I'd held him once, I would not feed him any mortal drug. But I little thought he'd make the effort to replace himself, either so that I'd not ken where he'd gone, or more like, so that there'd be a station for him in the other world. He had a certain cunning; I'll grant him that."

"But if you knew . . . " Phllip[2] began. "Why didn't you. . . ?" He found himself blushing.

She patted his hand. "Certes, I could ha' transported you incontinently to badge my mate's facinorous stratagems, save that on the sudden—I'll coyly confess—I took a fancy to you. And so I'd as lief keep the bargain the way it stands if you subscribe and, seeing that y'have no escape from this realm, owing not even so much of the rudiments of sorcery that my old fere had, y'needs must concur."

"Needs must," Philip[2] agreed. "As a matter of fact, Dolly, I think you're a most attractive Woman and I *want* to stay. But speaking of sorcery, haven't you noticed all the crocuses lying about? I—"

There was a dull boom in the distance. The room shook slightly. Both Philip[2] and Perkin jumped in the air, clutching each other.

"There goes the princeling's spell!" Dorothea observed complacently. "The brat took so long, I'd well-nigh forgot it. I knew not that we'd hear the hurley this far distant. Methinks he chose his moment well—and caught his family with their spells down."

She dabbed at her eyes with a handkerchief. "But 'tis meet that I show decent grief—for we were kin. Aye, Philip, I have royal blood coursing in these veins and if my charm was as thorough as 'twas loud, y'rnay find yourself of higher estate in this realm than e'er you fantasied!"

Philip[2] was aghast, but palace intrigues were an important part of history. Maybe he could get accustomed to them. He hiccuped. After all, others did.

VII

'Twas pleasant, Philip[1] mused, as he gazed out the window at the twinkling street lanterns and above them at the black sky stelled with the same luminaries as lit his own realm, to be able to see what lay outside by looking through a crystal pane 'stead of into a crystal ball. For to use contrivance for something that should be unstudied detracts from its natural pleasance. This was a natural world, not a very wise one, mayhap—but then he was not an absolute genius himself.

He sneezed. "I must apply to tb'apothecary for those marvelous powders of which you spoke," he said sheepishly to Dora. At first he had refused to let her procure them for him, but now he had altered his opinion. Very likely, a local disease would be more susceptible of cure by a local remedy. He must not be proud-stomached about the native magic if he planned to live as a native himself.

"*Druggist,* dear," Dora said. "Not *apothecary.*"

"*Druggist,*" he repeated obediently.

They were sitting side by side on the couch, holding hands as if they were courting, which in a manner of speaking they were.

"Philip," she asked, "what are we going to do if Philip—if the other Philip—comes back?"

He caressed her tenderly. "I've been a-musing on that very question mine own self," he murmured, "for I'd be right loath t'have him change places with me—again,"

"And *I'd* be right loath—I wouldn't want him to, either. Philip—" she rested her head on his shoulder "—could you—that is, is it possible for you to make a trip to that other world and come back here?"

He sighed. "Unfortunately, I cannot, sweet. I ha' not told you, for I did not want you to despise me as a drumbling wretch—"

"I'd never, never think of you as that!" she said fervently.

"By mischance, I lost the spell which would enable me to return."

"But how can you lose a spell?"

"Th'ingredients of the magic powder which I use along with the incantation—I had them in a phylactery about my neck and somehow I lost 'em. Oh, well." He patted her hand. "I ha' no need to go back."

"Would you have gone back before if you'd had them?" she asked. "Is that the only reason you're staying, because you can't go back?"

"By my troth, no! Have I not told you? Ever since I glimpsed you in my crystal, my only thought has been to make you mine own?"

"Yes , you've *told* me," Dora murmured. "I wish I knew what to believe. Wait a minute." She quitted the room. He could hear her heels clicking on the stairs. What pretty thing was the wench up to?

She was back eftsoons. "I don't know whether I'm doing the right thing, Philip." And she gave him his lost phylactery.

He looked at the small velvet bag in amazement.

"I took it off your neck the first night you were here," she explained.

"It did smell so! I thought it was an asafetida bag or something. And you never seemed to miss it. Lucky I didn't throw it away."

He took it in his hand. "Wench," he asked, "are you certain sure you didn't know what 'twas?"

"How could I know, Philip?"

"There is no possible way," he mused, "and yet sometimes I wonder whether I am wrong in thinking the magic of this realm is primitive—that mayhap it's so devilish deep, it lies beyond my braining."

"Don't be silly, Philip," Dora giggled. "There is no magic in this world. Nobody with any intelligence believes in such a thing. I know you have magic, of course, but it's all right for another plane of existence."

"Aye—er—yes," Philip[1] said. "When you put it that way, everything becomes crystal clear."

"Now that you have the spell," she asked, "will you go back?"

"But I vowed to you, sweet mouse, that I have no wish to return. I wish but to bide with you."

"Good. Then you've *got* to go back."

He stared at her in total bewilderment. "As long as I wish not to return, I must? The sense of it eludes me."

"Don't you understand?" she pursued. "You've got to go back and make sure the other Philip can't possibly come here. That's the only way we can be safe."

"'Tis a sad thing to confess," he said dolefully, "but my artifices are no match for Dorothea's. If she tires of the wight, she would send him here and me there despite aught I did to thwart her."

She looked thoughtful. "Maybe you could—well, sort of kill him. Without," she added hastily, "really killing him, I mean. You know, use your magic to put a spell on him or something."

"Which Dorothea would negate, if she wished, with scarce a moment's thought."

"All right, then," she said firmly. "Get rid of him or have somebody do it."

He gawped at her. So sweet a lady and so sanguinary! Almost she minded him of Dorothea. But all the sex had much in common and bloodthirstiness, he supposed, was a feminine trait.

"Why," he protested in agitation, "I could ne'er do't! He is my own person, my very counterpart! If I slay him or have Him slain, 'twould be the equal of suicide!"

"It's nothing of the sort," she insisted. "I know him better than you do and the two of you are not a bit alike, any more than this—this Dorothea person is like me! Besides, she's probably making his life wretched and it would only be putting him out of his misery. And not only that, why should we live in constant fear that he'll come back?"

"Perhaps he'll never find the way," he suggested hopefully.

Dora snorted. "She'll show him, never fear. She'll want to get you back and she'd know the best way to do it would be to send him here to mess up everything. I know these slick women—always up to nasty tricks. She won't be satisfied till she dumps him back on me."

Of course she was right. Dorothea would be seeking ways and means to retrieve him. 'Twas the Devil's own problem to solve and he mauled his mind to find a solution.

"I have it!" he cried, inspired. "This is not the only realm. Why should not your erstwhile spouse choose another? I can transport him from one t'other until he finds one as much to his liking—" he embraced her tenderly—"as this one is to mine."

"It's too good for him," she objected. "And how could we be *certain* Dorothea wouldn't find him in one of those places and send him here so she could get you back?"

"Ah!" he said cunningly. "I may unwitting transport him to a realm where he'd be devoured by wild beasts or savages. But then the blame would not rest on me. Would you have a husband bowed down by guilt, liefest?"

"I suppose not," she said reluctantly. "Men always have such annoying consciences when it comes to something they don't really want to do." She twisted in his arms. "Philip, when will you go back? Tonight?"

"A-yes, I could do that," he agreed. "But first I must consult my crystal to see what they're doing."

"You have a crystal ball with you?" she squealed. "And you never showed me? I think you're *mean!*"

She peered intently into the glass with him. "*He* seems to like her very much," she said drily. And indeed the two were seated companionably enough—even amorously—before the fire, with a bottle of the best Canary before them. Philip[2]'s arm was around Doll's waist; 'i faith, Dorothea's love potion must have been a mortal strong one.

"Is that her?" Dora queried. "I don't think she's so bad-looking."

Philip[1] strained his eyes. Was that in truth Doll? Why, the wench had bedizened herself, incarnadined her lips and cheeks and braided her blazing locks atop her head! And the flaunts she was wearing, cut in the accustomed style of the amorous ladies of the town and fashioned out of Cyprus, which, despite the stitcheries upon it, still offered little substance to block the questing eye. The wantom jade—she had never bedecked herself in such wise for him! Were she not so latten thin, y'might almost term her handsome.

"You need barnacles, my sweet," Philip[1] said, kissing Dora's cozy plum-cheeked face, "for she's a monstrous ill-favored besom. Clever, no doubt, but that's all."

"You don't like intellectual women, do you, Phil?" Dora asked, snuggling up to him.

"My dear," he said, "I loathe them."

"Go back now and tell him he mustn't come here ever," she commanded, "or else you'll send him where he'll like it even less than where he is now."

"Will't not wait until the morrow?"

"Now!" She looked up at him, dimpled. "Pretty please."

"Oh, very well." It looked as if, one way or another, he was born to be ruled by a woman.

Philip[1] took the precaution of remaining invisible so that he might not be espied by Dorothea afore he could draw his counterpart aside for parley. He wanted to run no risk of encountering Doll, for he knew she'd be hot to get him to return.

As he gazed at the reechy tapestries and Turkey cushions of his quondam room and breathed in the rich aroma of its vapors, he could not restrain a half-sigh of regret. 'Twould take some little time t'alter the appointments of his new realm according to his inclinations. But Dora was a sweet and complaisant lady so far. She'd fall in with all of his desires.

"What ails you, Philip?" Dorothea demanded, and Philip[1] well-nigh replied until he saw that her remark was addressed not to him but to the other. He was much put about to hear that his shrill-gorged Dorothea now cooed as gently as a dove. "D'you not love me?" she asked. "You said y'did not so many minutes agone. Are you so changeable then?"

"I do love you, Dolly," the hilding said in a voice like the lowing of an ancient cow. He took her hand in this. What was that upon her talons? Philip[1] squinted. Colored varnish, as he lived and breathed. Marry, Doll was festinate at picking up the wanton tricks of another realm! "More than I ever did Dora," t'other Philip whined. "But there's no place for me in this world."

"There's no place for you in your own world either, scroyle!" Philip[1] thought, "as you'd discover with a wanion, were you t'attempt a return passage."

"How so?" Doll asked, still addressing Philip[2]. "Will y'not be my loving husband, t'aid and comfort me and help in my work? Is that not sufficient honor for you? Moreover, you can assist me with my magicking. Why, you learned the spell for conjuring up croci in no time. I was monstrous proud of you."

"Were you really, Dolly?" Philip[2] asked, brightening.

"Of a certainty I was proud. Why, my sometime spouse could not pick up a spell so festinately. I did but instruct him in a few of my simpler mysteries, and wi' such small skills the drumbling varlet set himself up as sorcerer."

"Why, the saucy ronyon!" Philip[1] thought indignantly. "I've forgot more about sorcery than ever she kenned. Simply because I was not able to get first honors, as she did by cozening the Board of Examiners . . . Od's pittikins, avaunt, Perkin!" he exclaimed in a hoarse whisper, for the cat, having descried an old companion, was rubbing against his trousers to show he was no fair-weather friend, digging his claws in the luxurious texture of the tweed and purring most melodious to show his pleasance.

He was mazed that the keen-witted Dorothea took no cognizance of the whoobub, and concluded that she was indeed bestraught—which would serve to explain so much of her fantastical behavior. Fancy-sick for that pallid snipe, push!

"Aye, liefest," Dorothea murmured, inclipping Pbilip[2]'s waist, "you'll abide at home and tend the house and help me with my spells and—" the wench actually blushed, unless Philip[1]'s eyes were enchanted—" haply our progeny."

"But—but—" Philip[2] protested, "I want to be something in my own right, as I was in my own universe."

"Oh, aye," Philip[1] thought. "A second-rate pedant—what dignity is there in that? Why, I ha' made you—or rather myself—a national figure of heroic proportions. Your whole world has fallen at my feet in abject admiration. Were you to return now, you'd find yourself in a pretty coil . . . And these wonders I have contrived with the 'small skills' the jade affects to despise. Why, I'd flee from existence to existence unto timeless infinity rather than return to you, Doll . . . !"

"'Honey mouse," Dorothea said, embracing the barefaced Philip[2] more tightly, "why can y'not understand that because the goal of man and the goal of woman differ, each cannot be equally worthy in his own right? Chew upon this if 'tis I who have the greater brain, 'tis you who have the kinder heart. And I, thinking with my brain, and you, loving with your heart—together, sweet consort, we'll form a pair that will hold sway over this world."

"Doll waxing sentimental!" Philip' thought incredulously. "Why, the wench has gone clean out of her wits! A rap over the costard with the ladle was ever more her fashion."

"D'you not apprehend, sparrow?" Dorothea asked. "If this existence is pleasing to you, 'tis because it expects naught of you save what lies within your natural powers. And you have powers that perchance you never dreamed of. My tricksy tutelage will make a second-rank wizard out of you—that's a grade higher than my spouse ever was."

"Gee, Dolly," Philip[1] said eagerly, "that would be wonderful. But do you think you can teach me?"

"Of a certainty I can, for y'are already half-trained as sorcerer."

"I'm a scientist," Philip protested.

"'Tis the same thing. What though your world's magic be of a rudimentary nature, still the important thing is that science or magic or whate'er you term it is your profession. Oh, I'll make a parlous wizard out of you, lad, never fear."

"I'd like that," Philip[2] said. "Experiments are so damned messy. And even if I got back, I'd never be able to accept science properly again, knowing that the same thing can be done so much more simply."

She smiled at him. "So you'll abide with me, chuck? I could compel your attendance. However, if you would return to your own dwelling and your own spouse, but say the word and I shall transport you—though it break my heart to do so."

"She could have gone after me!" Philip[1] said to himself wrathfully. "She could ha' pursued me to the next realm and plucked me forth like a gilly-flower, had she been so minded. She didn't want me, the strumpet! I've a mind to return to her now, even though it be only out of spite!"

Philip[2] looked up at Dorothea. "Dolly, you've convinced me. It'll take me a little time to get adjusted, though."

"Of a certainty," she agreed. "And I'll assist to the best of my not inconsiderable skill."

"The conditioning I've received from my former environment will be hard to overcome," he went on. "There are certain deep-rooted psychological factors."

"I'll brew you a potion that'll clean wipe away all conditions and psychological factors and suchlike evil spells," she murmured tenderly. "And now one kiss, my love," she added. "I have a small matter to which I must attend ere we seek our couch. There's a maggot crept into this room from the woodwork and I needs must fordo the miserable creature, else the house will be crawling with vermin."

"Yes, dear," Philip[2] said, kissing her.

Dorothea had never bussed *him* in such wise, Philip[1] thought resentfully as he followed her into an antechamber.

"Make yourself apparent, wretch!" she cried in her familiar shrill tones. 'Twas evident she'd not forgot her rope-tricks, after all. "Once a jolthead, ever a joltbead! Did't not occur to you, mome, that enchanting the sense of sight so that none could see you had no effect upon my other senses? I could hear your sniffles whooping through the room like the wheezing of an asthmatic ass. What ails you—an ague? Th'ailments of another realm are monstrous plaguey. But you'll not die of this one, coistrel, more's the pity!"

A fine thing—a dutiful wife would have been a-cosseting and a-posseling of him . . . But then Dorothea had never been dutiful and, if things went according to stratagem, she was no longer his wife. Still, she might have brewed him a remedy for old time's sake.

"And then poor fond Perkins rubbing 'gainst your legs!" she went on. "Marry I knew not whether to laugh or weep! Know y'not, fool, that I can sense whenever an intruder enters the room by the tingling of my toes—all enchantment notwithstanding?"

"I'd heard of this power peculiar to those of the blood royal," he admitted grudgingly, "but I'd not believed it."

"Well, you can believe it now!" She let her eyes course over his exterior and shrieked with laughter. "What manner of strange apparel are you wearing, fool? In truth, y'look the veriest ape."

"Your Philip, chewet," he retorted, stung, "is garbed in the same fantastical dress, for indeed th'attire I flaunt is his very own. Yet he seems not amiss in your eyes."

"His vestures accord well with his form," she said, "though I intend to clothe him in velures and gold as befit his estate. But such garb as he affects sorts not well with you, for it reveals entirely too much of the person for a cavallero as gorbellied as yourself.

He swallowed his wrath just in time, remembering he wished to placate her. "My customary habit would ha' caused tongues to clack in t'other realm," be replied mildly. "But what estate is't you speak of? For fustian was ever good enough for me."

"Philip," she said, roundly changing the subject, "y'know I'm the better sorcerer."

"You some doctrine that I have not," he acknowledged. "For I was denied th'opportunity to do graduate work, sith I'm not one to blandish the Dean."

"I could send you back to t'other world any time I listed."

"Agreed, now that I apprehend you know the spell."

"Or I could send you to any realm of existence I fancied, including some of surpassing unpleasantness."

"You could, dear heart, you could. But would you?" He looked at her with sorrow as palpable as he could make it. "I, your own dear spouse for nigh onto a decade. After the tender memories we've shared together, would you use me so scurvily?"

"We were wedded when we were too young to know our own minds," she said. "Consider, you were but two-and-twenty and I a year your junior."

"Yes, there was the difference of a year atween us," he replied.

"Philip," she said, "I have become much affected, I must agnize, of this fellow you substituted for your own uncouth self. I know you've come back to me, but you've played your knavish tricks once too often. I'll have none of you."

"Verily?" Philip[1] groaned. "Oh, this is indeed a cruel blow!"

Her voice was almost soft. "I know it must be, Philip. But I think I can be happier with him than ever I was with you. If you had any affection for me, there should still remain some small desire in you for my welfare."

"Dolly," Philip[1] said in broken tones, "I must avow I am not made of adamant and you have moved me more than I can say. Take him—I hope you'll both be very happy."

He buried his face in his hands and managed to shake his shoulders convincingly.

"I'm glad you're putting a good countenance upon't," she replied with gentleness. "And after all, remember, Philip, 'tis you I love, but slightly altered."

"'Twill serve to comfort me in the long, lonely reaches of the night," he sighed, wiping his eyes on his sleeve.

"The law will accept this Philip as my husband. It must, for I am . . . However, be that as it may. I do not know whether you found the wench that was my Philip's wife pleasing. He says she is not."

"Why, the . . . ! Why, she's well enough," Philip[1] said cautiously. "Naught to compare wi' you, Doll—somewhat sunburned and mean of height—but well enough."

"So, Philip, I give you your choice—either you journey back to my Philip's realm or to any realm of your choice. So long as y'do not stay here, 'tis importless to me."

Philip' drew a long breath. "In such case, I think I'd as lief return to the one I have just quitted. 'Twould be a prodigious burden upon Dora—that's the name of the wench there—were her husband to—keep a-altering and a grief were he to disappear entirely . . . for she's a poor fond dame who needs a man to lean upon. I must think of her. Perchance I have thought overlong and overmuch of my own sweet self."

"Philip," Dorothea said, "I think the change has made a better man of you."

"Aye, Doll," Philip[1] agreed, readying himself for the return journey and Dora's waiting arms. But she was looking speculatively past him to where Philip[2] awaited. "D'you think," she wondered aloud, "there might be still better in other realms?"